She blinked, quizzical. "Levi? Is that really you?"

He bobbed his head. "Gail? Why, you look pretty as I remember."

"It's been ten years," she said, brushing off his compliment. "People change."

Sensing displeasure in her voice, he dropped his gaze. "I know I left without saying anything. I should have stayed in touch."

Launching a frown, Gail folded her arms. "That's a poor way to say you're sorry."

He toyed with the hat in his hand. "I guess I owe you all an apology."

She offered a tight nod. "You do."

When Levi had run away, she'd been on the cusp of fourteen. His departure had crushed her. He didn't know it, but he'd taken her heart with him.

Now he was back.

And so were the feelings she'd believed she'd let go of...

Like the Amish, **Pamela Desmond Wright** is a fan of the simple life. Her childhood includes memories of the olden days: old-fashioned oil lamps, cooking over an authentic wood-burning stove and making popcorn over a fire at her grandparents' cabin. The authentic log cabin Pamela grew up playing in can be viewed at the Muleshoe Heritage Center in Muleshoe, Texas, which was donated to the city after the death of her grandparents.

Books by Pamela Desmond Wright

Love Inspired

The Cowboy's Amish Haven

Visit the Author Profile page at Harlequin.com.

The Cowboy's Amish Haven

Pamela Desmond Wright

LOVE INSPIRED
INSPIRATIONAL ROMANCE

LOVE INSPIRED®
INSPIRATIONAL ROMANCE

Recycling programs for this product may not exist in your area.

ISBN-13: 978-1-335-75874-3

The Cowboy's Amish Haven

Copyright © 2021 by Kimberly Fried

This edition published by arrangement with Harlequin Books S.A.

For questions and comments about the quality of this book, please contact us at CustomerService@Harlequin.com.

Love Inspired
22 Adelaide St. West, 40th Floor
Toronto, Ontario M5H 4E3, Canada
www.Harlequin.com

Printed in U.S.A.

And the king said unto the man of God,
Come home with me, and refresh thyself,
and I will give thee a reward.
—*1 Kings* 13:7

For Tamela Hancock Murray, who believed.

For Melissa Endlich, who made it happen.

Acknowledgments

I would like to thank my fellow writers
and buddies who are always there to encourage
and cheer me on when the going gets tough.

Sara Reinke, Sascha Illyvich, Claire Matturro,
Vanessa Hawthorne, Marie Blackwood,
Sherri K Briles, Christie M Allen,
Ang & Sherry Baca.

I'd also like to thank my mother
for suffering through endless revisions
and telling me everything I wrote
was good (even though it often wasn't).

Love you all!

Chapter One

Rubbing tired eyes, Levi Wyse breathed a sigh of relief. Days of hard travel were finally nearing their end. Mile after mile disappeared beneath the tires of his truck.

Goodbye, Montana. Hello, Texas.

Gaze focused on the road, he drummed his fingers on the steering wheel. To stay awake for the last leg of the journey, he'd slammed down a few cups of coffee. Buzzed on caffeine and adrenaline, he felt tiny ignitions spark off his nerve endings. If only his blood didn't feel so hot and his skin cold as ice.

Sleep. All he wanted to do was close his eyes and hibernate for a week.

Levi glanced at the child sleeping in his car seat. Seth stretched out as much as the cramped interior allowed. Thankfully, his son could bunk out anywhere. Teddy bear locked in the crook of one arm, Seth mumbled in his sleep.

Emotion squeezed Levi's throat. The little guy was trying to be a trouper, but it was clear the last few months of hard travel had taken a toll. Instead of being dragged down the road, the child needed to be settled in a stable, normal routine.

Levi blinked to clear away the blur overtaking his vision. The white lines dividing the highway were running together. Pressing his fingers against his thudding temple, he pulled in a breath. To say he felt terrible would be an understatement.

He eased down the window and tipped back his head, allowing the cool night air to caress his stubbled face. The cobwebs and shadows inhabiting his mind thinned, but not enough to chase away his headache.

Feeling a twinge in his neck, he rolled his shoulders to loosen knotted muscles. His skin felt tight. A tremble threatened to overwhelm his fragile composure.

He had to find somewhere to pull over before he wrecked the truck.

Insides knotting, Levi clenched the wheel tighter. His destination was still miles away. He'd planned to find a place to set up the RV in Burr Oak. That wasn't going to happen. He was too tired to keep going.

A familiar landmark came into view.

Recognition seeped into his fogged mind. The ranch he'd worked at as a teenager was just a few miles away.

Maybe the Lord was watching out for him after all.

Even though he hadn't had contact with Samuel Schroder or his family in ages, he was pretty sure the man would let him park his camper for a day or two. As he remembered it, Samuel was always up before the sun, so pulling in early should not be a bother. Maybe he could even pick up some work doing odd jobs around the property to pay back the favor.

The next rodeo he planned to compete in was still a

week away, so he'd have some time on his hands. Spending a little time in one place for a while would be nice.

Stirring, Seth opened his eyes. "Are we there yet, Daddy?" Yawning, he squeezed his stuffed bear tighter.

Sucking back a sigh, Levi brushed a few stray locks off his son's forehead. *"Ja."* Unwilling to risk falling asleep behind the wheel, he decided to head for the nearby ranch. "We're getting close."

Gail Schroder sprinkled flour over the cutting board and flattened out a ball of sourdough. Every morning she baked fresh biscuits, a task in which she took great pride. True, the recipe was a common one, but she'd made it her own with a few special ingredients.

As was her custom, she had risen before the sun. Dressing quietly, she eased down the stairs, preparing to wrangle the ancient monstrosity dominating the kitchen. Feeding a fair amount of wood and kindling into its belly brought the old cast-iron beast to life.

Breakfast was her first task. Fire stoked, she started an old-fashioned coffee percolator. The scent of burning oak and a dark roast brew filled the air with a delicious aroma.

Gail pressed out a dozen biscuits and brushed the tops with home-churned butter mixed with honey from the beehive. After opening the oven, she slid the first batch inside.

Stepping back, she swiped a hand across her perspiring brow. The old stove took no time at all to heat the first floor. As was the layout of most Amish homes, the kitchen, dining room and living room all inhabited a single large living space.

A rectangular wooden table covered with a pretty,

ivory-colored lace cloth waited for stoneware dishes handed down through generations. The long picnic-style table with chairs on each side provided plenty of room for everyone.

A single wooden chair sat at its end, reserved for the man of the family.

Gail's head dipped as her eyes misted. The painful grip on her heart grew tighter, burrowing deeper. Oh, how she missed her *daed*. Her *mamm*, too, was gone, leaving only herself and her younger sisters.

Gail glanced out the nearby window. The yellow-pink sliver appearing over the horizon was widening and brightening. Out in the henhouse, the rooster's sunrise song cracked the silence of the night.

A new day was dawning, and a long list of chores waited. Cleaning, gardening, mending, tending the chickens, rabbits and goats that provided fresh eggs, meat and milk were just a few of the things that needed to get done.

The unexpected odor of charred bread and over-perked coffee singed her nostrils.

"Oh no!"

Gail snatched a flannel potholder and lifted the percolator. Liquid bubbled out of the spout. After setting the scorched thing aside, she fished the biscuits out of the oven. Twelve black circles greeted her eyes.

I ruined everything.

Biting back a sob of frustration, Gail stared at the disaster. Her emotions scattered in a thousand different directions. Without warning, her mask of stoicism and strength fell away, revealing deep cracks in her composure.

Grief. Loss. Confusion. They came at her from different directions, pecking at her like hungry ravens attacking carrion.

A tear rolled down her cheek. And then another.

Had her morning been normal, her *daed* would have been sitting in his chair, coffee in hand, Bible in front of him.

Gail swiped away her tears with a trembling hand. Since his passing, the family had left his Bible undisturbed. No one could bear to move it.

Walking over to the window to let in the morning breeze, Gail pulled in a hearty breath. Her focus was slowly returning.

Catching a glimpse of her reflection in the depths of the glass, she pulled a face at her image. Critical of her looks, she believed her eyes too wide set, and her mouth too generous. Her nose and cheeks were splattered with too many freckles. And no matter how tightly she wound her bun, a few brown curls always managed to escape her *kapp*.

I never look well put together, she thought, tucking her hair back into place.

A heavy rap at the back door interrupted her thoughts.

"Miss Gail?" a male voice called.

Gail recognized Ezra Weaver's voice. A visitor so early in the morning didn't bode well.

"Oh, please, Lord," she murmured. "I can't handle more bad news." Being the boss was hard. Harder than she'd ever imagined. She had a multitude of problems, the least of which was the ranch manager who had just quit without a word. Overseeing the homestead, which included the breeding and sale of Longhorn cattle, was considered a man's work. Now she had no guide, and no idea what to do.

Another knock sounded, louder and more insistent. "Anyone there?"

Glancing down, Gail sighed over the mess. She was hot and perspiring, her dress was wrinkled, and her apron stained by spluttering coffee grounds and flakes of dough.

"Just a minute!" She slid back the chain and unlatched the bolt.

Ezra Weaver waited outside. Mechanic, plumber, welder and jack of all trades, he'd come to work for the family seven years ago. If it broke, he fixed it. His wife, Ruth, took care of the cowboys, cooking and cleaning for the men who lived in the bunkhouse. An *Englischer*, he smoked a lot. Gail tolerated his bad habit because he was an honest man and a good worker.

"*Guder mariye*, Mr. Weaver." Gail angled the door so he could step inside. "Please, come in."

Battered straw hat in hand, Weaver offered an apologetic nod. "Sorry to disturb you so early, ma'am."

Gail smiled. Whatever he threw her way, she wouldn't flinch. It was up to her to make the decisions now, she thought, then sent up a silent prayer. *Gott, please help me make the right ones.*

"Not at all," she said. "How can I help you?"

"I'm not the one needin' your attention," Ezra Weaver drawled before jerking his thumb in a vague direction. "There's a man down by the gate, and he's askin' to see your daddy."

Surprised, Gail laughed in disbelief, then sobered when she realized Ezra Weaver was serious. Puzzled, she shook her head. Why would someone be asking to see her father? Three months had passed since Samuel

Schroder's death. Burr Oak was a small town. Surely word had gotten around by now.

She was curious as to who would make the inquiry, and why they had come so early in the morning. Visitors were not common. Weeks might pass before they saw a soul aside from family or hired hands.

"Do you know who it is?"

Ezra shook his head. "Nope. I ain't never seen him before."

"Did he say what his name was?"

"He said Samuel would know him."

"Well, in that case, I guess I need to find out what he wants."

"I'll come, too," Ezra Weaver offered.

Gail untied her apron and hung it on a peg by the door before brushing the flour off the front of her dress. She wanted to look mature, in control. Her efforts only added more smudges and wrinkles.

She opened the door and stepped outside. Nudged by the wind, the hanging chair on the veranda creaked.

Pulling back her shoulders and leveling her chin, Gail walked down the steps. Gravel crunched under her heels as she marched toward a white fence with a wrought iron gate that kept people from entering the property. Ezra Weaver dutifully followed.

Pasting a polite smile on her face, Gail peered through the bars. *"Guder mariye,"* she said, out of habit using the language she'd been raised to speak.

The driver slid out of his truck. Tall and blond, he was dressed in jeans, boots and a plaid checkered work shirt with the sleeves rolled to the elbows. He looked like any cowboy roaming the open plains.

"Guder mariye," he returned, tipping the wide brim of his straw hat.

Her brows rose. His pronunciation was decent enough. "Can I help you?" she asked, switching to English.

The visitor shifted to get a better view through the gate. His gaze widened, as did his grin. "Gail? You sure grew up."

The fine hairs on the back of her neck rose. "Do I know you?"

The man took off his hat, giving her a better view of his face. A blond layer of stubble roughened his skin. "Well, I hope so."

Gail searched for recognition. His eyes were his most arresting feature. Irises the shade of an icy arctic lake sparkled. Wry amusement slanted his mouth.

Noticing her lag, he took a step closer. "It's Levi," he prodded. "Levi Wyse."

Blood drained from her face. No. It couldn't be. This man didn't look like the boy she remembered. A thin scar marred his right cheek, and the slightly crooked set of his nose indicated a break or two throughout his life. His skin was deeply tanned, and small lines etched the outer corners of his eyes. A few character lines touched his mouth and chin. His voice, too, was deep, but mellow.

An image she'd put away long ago flashed across her mind's screen. When she'd last laid eyes on Levi, he'd had a huskier build and still wore his hair in the bowl cut favored by most Amish men. Now he had the lean and hard frame of a working man, and his hair was cut in the sleek combed-back style favored by most Texas cowboys. He'd replaced the clothes he'd once worn as one of the Plain folks with Western-style wear. Shedding his past, he'd gone *Englisch*.

She blinked, quizzical. "Levi?" Saying his name felt odd. "Is that really you?"

He bobbed his head. "Gail? You look as pretty as I remember."

"It has been ten years," she said, brushing off his compliment. "People change."

He dropped his gaze. "I know I left without saying anything. I should have stayed in touch."

Launching a frown, Gail folded her arms. "That's a poor way to say you're sorry."

He toyed with the hat in his hand. "I guess I owe you all an apology."

She offered a tight nod. "You do."

When Levi ran away, she was on the cusp of fourteen. His departure had crushed her. He didn't know it, but he'd taken her heart with him.

Now he was back.

What did he want?

An awkward silence widened the distance between them.

A boy with tousled blond hair popped up on the passenger's side. Rubbing sleepy eyes, he looked around in confusion.

"Dad," he called in a panic. "Daddy!"

Walking to the passenger side, Levi opened the door. "I'm here, calm down, son."

Gail caught a glimpse of the child as Levi unbuckled his car seat and lifted him out. "Your *boi*?"

Pride sparked in Levi's gaze as he cradled his son in his arms. "*Ja*. This is Seth."

Curiosity prodded. "And your *ehefrau*?"

Levi's mouth twisted wryly. Unease shadowed his eyes. "I'm sorry to say that Seth's mom isn't with us anymore."

Gail stood for a moment, locked in surprise.

Oh, no! How unkind of her to allow past resentments to control her emotions. Instead of welcoming him, she'd greeted him with an icy heart.

Shame filled her.

Unlatching the gate, she stepped through. "Forgive me for treating you so badly. Welcome home, Levi."

Chapter Two

"Thank you for inviting us in. I promise we won't stay long," Levi said as he and Seth followed Gail into the house.

"Please, sit." Face breaking into a smile of good humor and grace, she gestured toward the waiting table. "Can I get you anything to drink? Tea? Coffee? Maybe Seth would like something, too."

Hanging his hat on a peg by the door, Levi settled his son in a chair at the table before taking a seat. "Coffee would be great. A glass of milk for Seth, if it's not too much trouble."

Cranky after their long trip, Seth squirmed impatiently. "I'm hungry, Dad."

"Seth, don't be rude." Levi looked to Gail. "Sorry. I haven't had time to get him any breakfast this morning. I'd planned to stop somewhere in town."

"Well, I certainly can't let my guests go unfed. I insist you both stay for breakfast." Reaching for her apron, Gail knotted the ties around her slender waist. "Let me get the child something to tide him over."

Attempting to rub the exhaustion out of his eyes,

Levi nodded gratefully. "That would be a real treat. Been a long time since I've had a home-cooked meal, so I am going to say yes."

"I remember you used to eat like you had a hollow leg. *Mamm* couldn't fill you up," she said as she opened a bread box. Slicing off a piece of sourdough she toasted it on top of the stove before adding butter and a smear of pure strawberry delight. Stopping to fill a stoneware mug with milk, she delivered the items to the table with a deft hand.

Abandoning his bear, Seth grabbed the toast and stuffed in a large bite. "Mmm," he said, smacking his lips.

Levi frowned. "Mind your manners, son."

Mouth stained with jam, Seth used his sleeve to wipe away the mess. "Sorry, Dad."

Levi rolled his eyes. "He didn't learn that from me."

A flicker of amusement passed over Gail's face. "Now don't be too hard on the *youngie*," she said. "A good appetite is a good sign he'll grow." She turned her attention to Seth. "Do you like eggs with bacon and hash brown potatoes?"

Seth bobbed his head appreciatively, licking sweet strawberry jam off his fingers. "Mmm-hmm," he said before gulping down a mouthful of cold milk.

Gail returned to the stove, emptying the coffeepot and discarding inedible pieces of charcoal welded to a pan. Whatever she had attempted to make earlier had turned into a disaster.

"Problem?"

"Not my best morning." Exasperation knotted her brow. "I've got a lot on my mind."

"Oh?"

Gail waved off his concern. "It's nothing," she insisted. "Let me get some fresh coffee going."

Filling the pot with cold water and home-ground coffee beans, she set it on the stovetop to heat before rolling out more sourdough with a deft hand. The scent of a strong Colombian roast soon filled the air.

As she was otherwise occupied with her task, Levi snagged a mug off the counter before claiming a pot holder. "May I?"

She lifted hands covered in flour. "*Ja*, help yourself."

He tipped the metal percolator over. No modern machine could beat coffee brewed over a wood fire.

Looking up from her dough, she eyed him. "I'd forgotten you were so tall."

Levi gazed down at her. Her features were strongly etched, and her eyes evenly spaced over the slope of a perfectly straight nose. Dusty freckles spattered her cheeks.

"Guess if I say you're pretty again, you'll slap me."

Her cheeks heated, going ten shades of red. Her mouth twisted wryly. "Flattery won't get breakfast on the table any faster." Biscuits rolled out, she slid the pan into the oven.

Levi took the hint, backing off. It probably was not right to be saying such words to her anyway. Surely she had a husband somewhere nearby? And he most likely wouldn't take to a strange man making eyes at his wife, no matter their past connection.

He sat at the table and added cream and sugar to the tarry brew before taking a hearty sip. He let his gaze wander. Throughout the living space, sturdy handmade furniture filled the rooms. Crocheted afghans covered the sofas. Beneath the vaulted ceiling, the floor was solid oak with a scattering of handwoven area rugs. White lace curtains framed wide bay windows.

Save for Gail, the kitchen was empty. Normally, the house would be bustling with activity. Now it was strangely quiet, almost tomblike.

Having finished his snack, Seth yawned. His eyes drooped, struggling to stay open.

"Do you mind if I lay Seth down?"

"Not at all."

Levi slipped his arms beneath his son and carried him to a nearby sofa. He put him down and snagged an afghan to lay it on the boy. While Seth napped, it would give him a chance to talk to Gail.

Little pitchers have big ears, he reminded himself.

"Is he *oll recht*?"

Levi returned to his chair, finishing his coffee. "He's just worn out. I think being on the road so much is grinding him down. Getting to be time for a break."

"Oh?"

"We just drove down from Montana for some events here in Texas," he explained. "There's one in Eastland this coming Sunday. Then we'll head to Fort Worth for the rodeo there at the end of the month."

A faint smile haunted her lips. "*Daed* said that was what you would do. Join the rodeo."

"I know Samuel wasn't crazy about the idea." He shrugged. "Just something I had to do, I guess."

Gail's expression tightened. "*Daed* did the best he could by you, Levi."

As he caught sight of Samuel's Bible, guilt gave him a sharp prod. "I guess he'll tell me that when I see him."

Gail sliced off a slab of bacon with a sharp knife and added it to a cast-iron skillet waiting on the stovetop.

The meat sizzled, sending out the enticing aroma of pork cured in applewood. "I guess no one's told you, but he isn't with us anymore."

Surprise lifted his brows. *"Mein beileid an sie und ihre familie."* His pronunciation was rusty, but his offer of condolences sincere. "When did he pass?"

"Three months ago."

"How?"

Her expression remained cautiously neutral. "Unexpectedly."

Levi felt a twinge at the back of his throat. As hard as the old man had been on him, Samuel Schroder was never unkind. Gruff, maybe, but that was his way. "I know that must have been hard on your *mamm*. How is she?"

Gail's lips momentarily flattened. "Cancer took her, shortly after you left."

More news he had not expected. Sarah Schroder had always treated him well, sharing an uplifting thought or an encouraging word whenever he was discouraged or felt out of place.

"They were both good people. It doesn't seem right they're gone."

"It was *Gott*'s will." Quiet resignation tightened her words. "We can only accept it and pray they are at peace."

Levi swallowed hard. Hands circling the large stoneware coffee mug, he tried to draw some comfort from its warmth. "How have your *schwestern* been?"

Gail's gaze lifted from her cooking. *"Gut.* They've gone to town to deliver the morning produce, but they will be back soon."

"They are all well, I hope."

"*Ja*. Rebecca is a teacher. She is engaged and will be marrying in November. Amity has a little shop of her own. Her homemade soaps and candles are popular with tourists."

Levi nodded. "The things she made were always too pretty to use."

"She's had a place in town for about two years now, and her business is starting to grow."

"Dare I ask about Florene?"

Gail rolled her eyes. "*Ach*, that girl. She's been trouble lately."

"Really?"

A rueful smile flicked across her lips. "Seventeen and thinks she knows everything. Right now, she's testing the waters of *Englisch* ways."

Leaning into the table, Levi brushed his fingers through his hair. "Been there, done that."

She eyed him. "I hope you will be honest if she asks you about your time away from Burr Oak."

"I've got a story or two I could tell," he said, but declined to elaborate. "And you? You are married now. *Ja*?"

Throwing up her hands, Gail made a scoffing sound. "Who has time to find an *ehmann* with all this to tend to on the ranch?" Claiming a fork, she deftly turned the frying bacon without missing a beat.

Levi had no chance to reply. A series of hard knocks hammered the front door.

"Well, aren't we popular today?" Frowning, she lifted the skillet off the stove. Setting it aside, she wiped her hands on a dishrag. "Who could this be?"

Levi shrugged. "Guess you'd better find out."

Gail straightened her *kapp* and smoothed her apron before greeting the visitor.

Glancing past her, Levi caught sight of the man standing on the veranda. Clad in an impeccably tailored three-piece suit, he looked to be a portly man in his late forties, with dark hair gray at the temples. His face was round and cheeks unusually ruddy for his pale complexion. His deep-set eyes peered through the rims of stylish gold wire-frame glasses. Beneath a thin, dark mustache, his lips compressed into a line. By the look on his face, he'd not come for a social call.

"Is this the Schroder property?"

Gail nodded. "Yes."

Levi bristled. Something was not right. Men in dark suits didn't show up out in the middle of nowhere in Texas to chat. Not wanting to pry into her business, he nevertheless turned an ear toward the conversation.

The stranger grumbled. "Even with a GPS, these county farm roads are confusing. I hate being out this early, but it was necessary."

"I'm sorry for the inconvenience. It is easy to get lost." Stepping back, Gail invited him in. "Come in, please."

Entering, the man didn't offer his hand or a smile. His features were guarded, his eyes intense in their perusal. "My name is Andrew Wilkins. I work in the loan delinquency department for the bank in Burr Oak. I was hoping you could explain why the mortgage payments haven't been made in the last three months."

"I—I don't understand."

Wilkins's gaze narrowed, as if she were a hardship he had to force himself to tolerate. "The payments on this property are ninety days overdue." Reaching in a pocket, he extended a white legal envelope. "Your notice of default is enclosed. This will be your final notice."

Puzzled, Gail accepted his offering. "I'm sure there's some misunderstanding, Mr. Wilkins. *Daed* never missed a payment."

"Samuel was always a good customer," Wilkins said. "We've never had any qualms loaning him money over the years. When he passed, we had every confidence his survivors would honor his debt."

"Of course, we intend to keep paying," she said with quiet determination. "We wouldn't cheat the bank."

"Then perhaps you might explain why the account the payments are debited from has not had adequate funds in months." Pausing, he gave a prod. "I sent out written notices, but no one responded."

Gail shook her head. "That's not right. We sent cattle to auction after *Daed* passed and collected over a hundred and fifty thousand dollars for their sale. That was at the beginning of March and should have been more than enough to carry us through next year. Our manager, Mr. Slagel, should have taken care of it. He always has."

Wilkins's lips pursed into a sneer. "No significant deposit has been made to that account for months. Certainly not anything close to that amount."

Gail visibly paled. The unopened envelope slipped from her fingers, but she didn't retrieve it. "Oh no…" Barely able to speak, she pressed shaking hands to her mouth.

Wilkins's brows rose. "Excuse me?"

She took a breath to steady herself. "Slagel must have taken the money."

"Now, hold on—" Andrew Wilkins held up a hand. "Are you accusing him of embezzlement?"

Seeing Gail flounder, Levi's protective instincts kicked in. Having followed the conversation, he didn't have to struggle to put together the story she was trying to tell. He didn't know who Slagel was, but he intended to find out what was going on.

Rising to his feet, Levi stepped up, towering over the shorter man. "She has no reason to lie." Hands fisted at his side, he moved to shield Gail. "If she says the man took the money, it's true."

Blinking behind the rims of his glasses, Wilkins huffed. "Excuse me. I don't believe I was talking to you."

Levi refused to back down. The man was a bully, and he was using his position to intimidate. He refused to be cowed.

"Well, you are now."

Wilkins sniffed. "And you are?"

"A friend of the family," Levi returned in a cool tone. "A knowledgeable man could easily forge a bill of sale on livestock and collect a check in his own name. I doubt anyone would have questioned it if he was someone people trusted." Unfortunately, the theft of cattle was common.

Peeved, Wilkins responded, "What do you mean *was*?"

Moving like an automaton, Gail retrieved the envelope. Her composure hung by a thread. "Mr. Slagel disappeared. I don't know where he went."

Unmoved, Wilkins leveled her with a stare. "What you have going on with Walter Slagel is a legal matter you'll have to settle with him," he snapped. "Regardless of the circumstances, you will still need to make restitution for the amount owed."

Levi bristled. "What if she can't?"

"Then the bank will foreclose." His unrelenting gaze scraped every inch of the room. "Of course, that will include the house. Samuel put the primary acreage up as collateral, so this entire property will go to the bank."

"You would take our home?" Gail asked, aghast.

Wilkins unleashed a snarky grin. "Unless you catch up, I certainly intend to."

Struggling to keep his expression neutral, Levi looked over the rude man who apparently no had problem treating people like dirt. The entire situation left a bad taste in his mouth. He'd never had a stomach for fighting, but there came a time when a man had to stand up and do what was right.

Angling his chin, he folded his arms across his chest and stared the agent down.

"No, you won't," he returned with calm precision.

Still unable to process what had just happened, Gail stood rooted to the spot. Shock buffeted her from all sides. Her ability to think, to speak, had deserted her. She could only stare, numb with dismay and disbelief.

Levi, on the other hand, didn't seem to be affected.

Taking control, he grabbed Andrew Wilkins by the elbow. Propelling the shorter man across the room, he escorted him out of the house.

"We'll be in touch," he said, shutting the front door with a slam. Deed done, he brushed his hands together with satisfaction.

Relieved, Gail forced herself to relax for the moment.

She gave him a grateful look. "Thank you for making him go, Levi."

"It was no problem. How could he come in here and speak to you like that?"

Gail's gaze dropped to the envelope in her hand. No need to open it. Wilkins had made it perfectly clear what the paperwork inside would say. "Does it matter? The bank is going to take our home if we don't catch up."

"Now, hold on. Don't panic just yet."

Her facade of composure cracked, revealing her fear. "How can I not?" A shiver curled up her spine, causing her to tremble uncontrollably. Her vision blurred, misting with tears.

Levi stepped forward, grasping her arms and giving her a little shake. "Just calm down and tell me what's going on. Who is this man you're talking about?"

"His name is Walter Slagel. *Daed* hired him last year to oversee the cattle operation. His health was beginning to decline, and he needed the help."

As she broke free of Levi's hold, guilt pummeled her. When her father had needed her most, she had let him down. In so many ways. At her age, she should have been married. A son-in-law might have been able to take the burden off her father's shoulders.

"You said Slagel was gone," Levi said, prodding for more.

"Yes. He packed his things and left a few days ago. Before that, all our ranch hands quit."

"They give any reason?"

An anxious sensation squeezed her insides. "They were upset because he was behind on payroll. They complained about having to wait for their money."

Levi's brows furrowed, and the lines between his

eyes deepened. "That doesn't sound right. There's no good reason to pay your crew late."

Dropping her gaze, Gail bit her lip. Through the last few weeks she'd had the strange feeling something was not right with Walter Slagel. He'd become secretive, brushing off her questions about the day-to-day operations of the ranch. Her inquiries about the cattle, the crew and the books had gone unanswered, leaving her with a bitter taste in her mouth. But there was no chance to speak with him as to why he wasn't doing his job. He vanished without a word.

Regret choked her as she looked back. She should have acted sooner, confronted Slagel when the chance presented itself. "I know I made mistakes."

A somber look darkened Levi's gaze. "Sounds like walking out was probably the best thing he did."

"I was planning to fire him and hire someone else." She lifted the crumpled envelope. "But how do I fix this? How do I run a ranch without any money?"

Levi fished the envelope from her fingers. Tearing it open, he unfolded the papers inside. "I am no expert, but I do know how banks work, and how ranching works. It isn't as dire as Mr. Wilkins made it sound."

Grateful someone had answers, Gail relaxed. If Levi had the knowledge to help her, she would listen.

"You want to tell me what's going on with the bank?" he prodded.

Lowering her gaze, she sighed. "A few years ago, *Daed* was offered the chance to buy some acreage from our neighbor, Abram Fletcher. Abram wanted to retire, and he offered a fair price for his land. *Daed* saw it as a chance to expand the herd because beef prices have been good and there is a high demand for Longhorn meat. Mr. Fletcher wanted to be paid in cash, so *Daed* borrowed the money."

Levi nodded. "And Samuel put up his own land as collateral?"

"Yes. I can't see how we can keep the property now."

"You would be surprised what you can accomplish when your back is against the wall. Where there is a will, there's a way."

"Really? Then there is a chance we won't lose the house?" Grateful, Gail reached out, laying a hand on his arm. "Oh, Levi, if you would help me through this trouble, I would be so grateful."

"I think I can advise you," he said but didn't have a chance to explain.

The sound of footsteps on pavement stone and a rustling of skirts filtered in through the open window over the kitchen sink.

"The girls are back from town," she said, and pressed a single finger to her lips. "For now, we will keep this between us."

Surprise registered on his face. "You're not going to tell them?"

Fresh anxiety knotted her insides. Deception was unforgivable, but for now she was determined to shield her younger sisters from the betrayal Slagel had committed against their family.

"Not yet." Gail thought fast and made a quick decision. Claiming the paperwork, she stuffed it deep into a pocket of her apron.

Chapter Three

Stunned by Gail's request, Levi watched as she hurried back to the stove. "Please, say nothing to my sisters until we have had a chance to talk further."

Moved by her desperate tone, he nodded. "Of course." How Gail chose to conduct her business was just that. Her business. An outsider with no ties to the property, he had no say one way or another.

The back door opened. Faces bright and cheerful, the Schroder sisters entered the house.

Catching sight of him, all three women went silent.

Bending to retrieve the biscuits, Gail pasted on a smile. "Look who's come to join us for breakfast."

Puzzled, the women stood silent. No one recognized him.

"It's Levi," Gail prodded.

Blinking myopically, Rebecca was the first to respond. "This is certainly a surprise." She squinted behind a pair of wire-frame glasses.

"Yes, I guess it is."

Rebecca's smile broadened to fill her face. "You've

been gone a long time." She offered a hug, brief but heartfelt.

"Didn't mean for it to be that way," Levi said, more than a little ashamed he'd never considered the feelings of others when he'd decided to run off. Through the three years he'd lived there, the girls had treated him decently.

"You've changed," Florene blurted in a robust, forthright manner. "You look so old now." Tiny and fragile, she barely touched five feet. Her features, like her frame, were delicately etched.

Hovering in the background, Amity elbowed her younger sister. Soft and doughy, she had a round face with expressive brown eyes and red cheeks. "Mind your manners," she scolded. "Just because it's on your tongue doesn't mean you should say it."

Florene blushed. "*Vergib mir*. I meant no offense."

Levi offered a smile. "None taken. I guess I've changed a lot."

"You have," Amity said.

"But we are glad to see you," Rebecca added.

Awakened by the commotion, Seth sat up, rubbing his eyes. "Daddy?"

The women lit up.

"But who is this *kleinen* I see?" Rebecca asked, giving a little clap. "Your *sohn*, Levi?"

If there were anything good and right in his world, his child was the reason. "This is Seth." Crossing to the sofa, he ruffled his son's hair.

Squirming, Seth dropped his head and buried his face. Since his mother's death, he'd become reticent around strange people, especially women. "Nooo," he murmured, barely loud enough to be heard.

Levi placed a hand on the back of Seth's neck, massaging lightly. "Please excuse Seth's manners. He's been cranky these last few days."

Finishing the bacon, Gail turned her attention to making the hash browns, adding grated potatoes to the hot bacon grease. While those cooked, she cracked several eggs into a bowl, adding a dash of butter, milk, salt and pepper, before whipping them into a froth. She poured the mix into a second pan. "A *gut* meal will fix him right up." Remarkably composed, she acted as if everything was normal.

Settling Seth back at the table, Levi tucked a napkin under his son's chin. "You mind your manners around these ladies, now."

Seth nodded. "Yes, Daddy."

"Anything I can do to help?"

"Sit down, Levi," Gail invited. "We've got this."

Greetings done, the conversation drifted as the sisters bustled around, helping get breakfast on the table.

"Who was that man in the car?" Rebecca asked. "He came tearing down the drive so fast I thought he was going to hit the buggy. Beryl was so frightened she nearly bolted."

"He's from the bank," Gail answered, speaking noncommittally.

"Why would he come to the house?" Amity asked.

"He said there was an issue with how Mr. Slagel was handling the ranch account," Gail said, carefully choosing every word. "I told him that man was no longer working here, and that I would take care of the problem. It's nothing."

Rebecca frowned. "It seems to me like the man did nothing after *Daed* died. Thanks to him, we lost the cowhands." Claiming the coffeepot, she filled mugs with the steaming hot brew. "I'm so glad Ezra and Ruth have stayed on, or we would have no one."

"I'm going into town as soon as I can," Gail said. "I'm going to post a notice for hire and take care of a few other things."

"You've had so much to do," Amity said. "I don't see how you've kept up."

Gail pursed her lips. "Not well enough," she said in a self-deprecating manner. Hash browns done, she piled them into a heap on a plate. The scrambled eggs soon followed. Next was the gravy, which she made up from a roux of bacon grease and flour. Adding milk, she mixed up a thick country-style gravy.

"I never liked him," Florene piped up. "His eyes were tiny, seemed dishonest." She set plates heaped with food on the table. Fluffy biscuits and the gravy followed.

"My goodness, you've outdone yourself this morning," Rebecca said, sitting and spreading a napkin neatly across her lap.

"There's enough for at least ten people," Florene said, eyeing the food on the table.

"Everything looks wonderful," Amity said.

Gail tucked in her skirt before taking a seat. "We've got two hungry men to feed," she announced. "I haven't had a chance to tell you everything, but Levi's offered to help me hire a few cowhands and advise me about the cattle." She raised a brow, giving him a look. "Aren't you?"

Levi's own brows rose. In a way, it was true. Gail had asked him for help. He couldn't very well say no. If nothing else, he owed the Schroder family a debt of gratitude. Samuel Schroder had put a roof over his head and food in his belly when he needed it most. The older man had also given him a steady profession, teaching the ins and out of keeping cattle.

Making a quick decision, he backed up her words.

"I'm happy to help out in exchange for a few home-cooked meals." He'd planned to ask if he could park his trailer on their property a few days anyway, so her request just cemented the deal.

"That's so generous of you," Rebecca said. "None of us know a thing about the cows."

Levi nodded. "Glad to lend a hand."

Giving him a grateful smile, Gail unfolded her napkin. "Would you say grace, Levi?"

Her request caught him off guard. He had not bowed his head over a meal in years.

Conscience gave him a kick. It wouldn't be right to sit at their table and not respect their ways. "I'm not—" Feeling strangely embarrassed, he gulped in a breath. "I'm not very good at praying anymore."

Rebecca smiled. "I always tell my students to just say what's in their hearts."

Levi looked around the table. Each nodded encouragingly.

"Please," Amity invited. "I know it's been a while, but there will always be a place here at the table for you and Seth."

A twinge touched his throat. "Thank you. I appreciate the welcome." He wished now he'd made an effort to stay in touch. A postcard or short letter. He believed that once he was gone the family wouldn't give him a second thought.

Rebecca added, "When *Daed* welcomed someone to

his table, they were always *familie*. It isn't blood that binds people together but love and respect."

Giving each of them a look, Levi stretched out his hands. Seth sat to one side of him, Gail to the other. His son's small hand easily accepted his grip, as did hers. Beneath his touch, her skin radiated warmth and acceptance.

Levi bowed his head and closed his eyes. Reaching back in his memory, he tried to recall the many meals he'd eaten at this very table. Then, Samuel Schroder had sat at the head of the table, a strong man who was humble enough to give thanks for the many blessings he received.

Pulling in a deep breath, he fought to keep his voice steady. Somehow the words came easily, naturally.

"Dear Lord, thank You for welcoming me back to this table. Please keep Your guiding hands over those who are here and help us remember those who have passed…"

"Amen," the sisters murmured when he was done.

Blessing over, everyone tucked into their meal.

After cleaning his plate, Levi exclaimed, "If I eat another bite, my pants will burst."

Wiping his mouth, he pushed his now-empty plate away. The food Gail had prepared was not just delicious, it was a downright feast. The meal he'd just eaten was all harvested from the gardens and livestock kept on the property.

"There's still some bacon and hash browns left," Rebecca said.

"What about another biscuit with jam," Florene suggested.

"I'd like more bacon," Seth piped up.

Levi frowned at his son. "Remember your manners," he reminded, using his stern dad voice.

Seth grinned. "More bacon, *please*."

Sitting next to him, Amity chuckled. "I think that child has hollow legs."

Gail added another slice of bacon to Seth's plate and then refilled his empty glass. "The *boi* has a *gut* appetite."

Levi let out a sigh. "Don't be greedy. You don't need a stomachache later."

Chewing a piece of bacon, Seth grinned. "It tastes good, Dad," he said before releasing a loud burp.

Levi groaned. Once Seth had gotten over his shyness, he'd become the center of attention. All the sisters doted on him, encouraging his tales of rodeo life to grow bigger and wilder with each telling.

"Please, son. There are ladies present."

Amity chuckled. "He's quite the little storyteller."

Having grown up around the rough-and-tumble atmosphere of the rodeo arena, Seth had gotten an earful. Like a parrot, he memorized and repeated much of what he heard. "Don't get him started, please. He can tell tall tales all day."

Readjusting her spectacles, Rebecca snickered. "Oh, he's harmless compared to some of my students."

The sound of the grandfather clock chiming from its place in the sitting room interrupted further conversation.

"Oh my! The time got away," Amity said, gulping down the last of her coffee. "It's already nine."

Rebecca pushed back her chair. "I've got to go. I promised Noel I would help him at the butcher shop today. One of his clerks is feeling unwell, and he's shorthanded. Now that school is out for the summer, it will give me something to do," she explained, hurrying to the foyer to gather her bags.

Amity also put some speed into her steps. "If the horse trots fast, we can make it into town in twenty minutes," she said.

The two disappeared, gone for the day.

Seeming in no hurry, Florene dawdled at the table. "I'm so tired," she yawned. "I could sit here all day."

Gail passed her youngest sister a stern frown. "Haven't I warned you about staying up late on the phone?"

Levi's brows rose. "Phone?"

"The *Ordnung* allows phones for business or emergency nowadays," Gail explained. "It is not for social media and communicating with boys."

Florene blushed bright red and dropped her gaze guiltily. "I was just texting a friend," she mumbled.

Gail's hands settled on her hips. "And putting off your work," she scolded. "Don't you have rabbits and chickens to feed?"

Florene slumped as if she carried the weight of the world. "I feel like I'm tied down," she complained, crossing her arms with defiance. "I want to go places and do something more than tend animals and work in the garden. Someday I'll live the way I want—like Levi did."

Levi held up a hand. "Don't be so quick to use me as an example."

"I wish I wasn't here," Florene pouted.

Lips pressed flat, Gail shook her head. "Be careful what you wish for," she countered. "The world out there isn't easy, and some people aren't as friendly as you'd like them to be. You might find yourself handed a slap instead of a smile."

Florene returned a typical teenager's moody expression. "I'll find out. My birthday will come soon, and you can't stop me."

Annoyance filled Gail's face. "While you're under this roof, you'll still do your chores and mind the way you were raised." Her tone brooked no argument.

Shoving away from the table, Florene tossed down her napkin. Expression stormy, she headed out the back door. The wooden screen clattered back against the door frame.

Watching her go, Gail bit her lower lip. "How can I deal with that child?"

"Looks like someone is going through a little rebellion," Levi chimed in.

Gail sighed with weary patience. "I don't know what's happened. She has been like this since *Daed* died. I've tried and tried, but I can't keep her in line."

"You've all been through a tough time," Levi said. "Losing a parent isn't easy, I know."

"I'm sorry. I'd forgotten you lost your own family when you were young," Gail said.

Levi's stomach tightened. He'd lost his parents and siblings in a single day. "You know as well as I do, the hurt never really goes away."

"You're right." Gail's face mirrored her feelings. "The wound heals but the scars are still on our hearts."

Having sat remarkably quiet, Seth piped up. "My mommy died," he announced matter-of-factly. "Daddy says she's in heaven." He tilted his head back. "I look in the sky, but I never see her."

Sorrow wove its way through Levi's memory. Now

five years old, Seth was too young to recall much about his mother, or her tragic passing.

"Mommy knows you're looking," he said, forcing a lightness he didn't feel. "Remember what I told you?"

"When I see rainbows, Mommy's smiling at me."

"What a nice thought, Seth." Bending over, Gail cleared the dishes off the table. "I think I'll borrow it, if you don't mind."

Seth nodded. "I like rainbows. They're pretty."

"I agree," Gail said. "Perhaps you'll draw us one. I believe Rebecca keeps extra paper and colored pencils on hand for her students. Maybe I can get them out for you later. Would you like that?"

Seth clapped eagerly. "Yes, please!"

"Let me finish my dishes and I'll find them."

Levi stood. "Can I help?"

"I've got it. You just sit and rest a bit." Piling the dishes in the sink, Gail ran hot water into the basin. "I'm sorry to hear about your *ehefrau*." Washing each dish carefully, she sorted and stacked them to put away.

"Thank you." Helping himself, Levi replenished his coffee. "Seth's mom passed a few years ago. Since then, it's been just him and me."

Sliding out of his chair, Seth began to fidget. "Can we go out and play, Daddy?"

"In a minute, son. The grown-ups need to talk."

"Why don't we take a walk outside?" Finished with the dishes, Gail shook out her rag. "I could use a breath of fresh air."

Levi set his cup aside. "Good idea. I need to stretch my legs and walk off this meal."

Seth bounced up and down. His blond hair stood on

end, looking as downy and fine as the fuzz on a baby chick. "Yeah!"

"Calm down, buddy. Let's not get too excited."

"It's nice to see some excitement around here for a change." Hanging her apron on a peg, Gail opened the screen. "Come this way."

Outside, the three walked down a cobbled path, each stone laid by hand and perfectly aligned.

The house nestled in the center of a copse of towering oak trees mixed with some cedars and pecan. Providing welcome shade in the summer, the trees offered a break from the fierce winds often whipping across the wide-open plains. Thick grass blanketed the yard, the type that greened up in the spring and took on a straw shade come winter's frost.

The backyard was a delightful place for children. A set of old-fashioned flat seats attached to ropes hung from sturdy branches. A playhouse perched among the branches of the sturdiest tree, accessible by a rope ladder. A patio overhung by an awning promised a cool place to spend the days when summer's heat chased everyone out of the house.

Seeing the swings, Seth ran ahead and climbed into a seat. His stubby legs pushed against the ground. Within seconds, he was soaring back and forth.

"Look at me!" he giggled hysterically. "I'm flying."

Worry touched Gail's expression. "Take it easy."

Levi couldn't suppress his smile. For the first time in months, a touch of joy had lightened Seth's mood. The kid rarely got a chance to play.

"I was planning to have Ezra cut them down," Gail explained. "No one's played on those in quite a few years."

"I'm glad you let them stay. Seth's having a ball." He glanced around, taking in the neatly fenced gardens and pens where domestic livestock roamed. "Gosh, it's like I was here yesterday."

The corners of her mouth widened. "You've been away so long. I wondered what you'd remember."

"I know it must seem like I was ungrateful for leaving, but I didn't mean it that way."

"I guess there comes a time when a man has to choose his own path and follow it."

"I was seventeen, and far from being a man," he corrected.

Looking around, a rush of emotions tightened his throat. Losing his parents at such a young age had cost him the security of a home and family.

Taking him in, Samuel Schroder had given him a foundation under his feet where he had, after a time, began to grow and thrive. The older man had treated him fairly, encouraging him to stay on.

As long as a man has a piece of ground under his feet, he's got a home, Samuel had often said.

When he was younger, the idea of living in one town his whole life sounded boring and dull. Now that he was a father, Levi recognized the wisdom behind Samuel's words. Like a tree, a man also needed to set down roots.

Abandoning the swing, Seth ran up. A wide grin split his youthful face.

"I like this place," he said, throwing his arms around his father's legs and holding tight as he looked up with bright eyes. "Can we camp here, Daddy? Please?"

Gail laughed. "Of course, you can. I insist."

Levi felt a tug on his heartstrings. Glancing down at Seth, he returned his gaze to her face. Despite her cheerful demeanor, he knew the bank agent's visit put a heavy weight on her spirit.

"I think that's a great idea, son," he said, and gave Gail a knowing wink.

Nodding, she offered a smile. "I'm thankful the Lord sent you today, Levi. It's an answered prayer."

Chapter Four

Seth skipped ahead as they walked across the barn-yard. The youngster was delighted with the variety of animals in their pens.

"Dad, look, there's bunnies and chicks!" Spotting a handful of pups trailing their mother, Seth clapped his hands. "And puppies!"

"I see, son, I see." Giving his head a shake, Levi rolled his eyes. "You'd think the boy hasn't ever seen animals before."

Halfway hiding her grin, Gail soaked in the child's delight. Like most self-sustaining properties, the ranch looked like a petting zoo. Goats, chickens, rabbits and a few milk cows grazed behind the safety of barbed wire fences. A handful of mutts lounged nearby, keeping an eye out for predators. A barn with a nearby corral housed the horses, a sturdy breed of cow ponies bred to work with cattle.

Blue-eyed like his father, Seth was small for his age, with fine, delicate features. A ball of energy, he ran around to take in all the sights.

"Anything small is cute." Basking in Seth's delight,

she laughed. "That's the appeal of babies. They are born adorable for a reason."

Levi guffawed. "Can't say I saw much adorable in the red, squalling baby Betheny delivered. Seth was born with a good set of lungs and he used them a lot when he was hungry, that's for sure."

His comment perked Gail's curiosity. This was the first time Levi had mentioned Seth's mother by name. She knew the boy's mother was deceased but didn't know what had happened, or when.

A myriad of questions crowded into her mind. The desire to know more gripped her harder, but she decided not to pursue the topic. It would be rude to go prying into his private business. If Levi had something to say, he'd say it.

Have patience, she counseled herself. As the Bible said, all would be revealed in its time.

Having chased down a puppy, Seth caught the squirming canine in a bear hug. The canine wiggled with delight at the attention, covering the boy's face with wet, sloppy kisses. "Oh, Daddy, he loves me!"

Levi's mouth curved upward in the tight half smile parents often gave their children right before the word *nein* rolled off their tongue. "Looks that way."

Seth trotted up. "Can I have him? Please, please!"

Levi reached out, ruffling the pup's downy fur. "I know you want a dog, but we don't have room for one in the RV."

Seth's face fell a mile. Fat tears welled in his eyes. "But…but…you told me we could get a puppy…" he blubbered, hugging the animal tight. Squeezed within an inch of its life, the pup yelped with displeasure.

"Son, I said not right now. When we get a house of

our own someday, we will look into it." Sighing, Levi bent and pried the dog out of his child's protective grasp. "Turn it loose before you hurt it."

The mutt hightailed it back to its mother, disappearing among its littermates. A low growl rolled over the mama dog's taut lips.

Seeing his dream dash away, Seth bawled harder.

A little embarrassed, Levi grimaced. "Sorry. Someone's still on the cranky side."

Unable to bear the disappointment in the boy's eyes, Gail knelt, coming down to his level. "The pup belongs to no one, so he can be yours if you want him," she said. "But since your RV is small, maybe you should keep him outside. And while you are here, you can play with him every day in the barnyard. Will that work?"

Tears drying up as fast as they had appeared, Seth reluctantly nodded. "Can I name him, too?"

"Of course." She glanced up at Levi. "Does that sound like a plan to you?"

Giving her a look, Levi lifted the brim on his straw hat, giving his forehead a rub. "I think you just bamboozled me into getting a dog, though I'm not sure how yet."

Seeing him smile with genuine delight, Gail felt a pulse deep in her heart. Its beat shifted from steady to double time, sending warmth through her veins.

Back when he was a teenager, nothing ruffled Levi. He was courteous to a fault. Whereas she would grumble when saddled with household chores she had no love for, Levi had always done as he was asked. He never argued and had completed his work with quiet contemplation.

Standing, Gail brushed at her skirt to straighten out

the wrinkles. No matter how much starch she put into the ironing, her dresses never failed to look like she wadded them up before putting them on.

"You never could say no."

A shrug rolled off his shoulders. "It's easier just to tell a woman *ja* and let her have her way. What is the old saying? 'Happy wife, happy life.'"

Looking into his rugged face, Gail felt a blush warm her cheeks. She dipped her head and folded her arms in front of her chest. If things had been different, if she'd been older, would she have had a chance of winning his heart? As it was, she was barely on the cusp of fourteen when he'd departed.

Blinking hard to still her racing mind, Gail pushed the unwelcome thought out. No matter which path she walked, the outcome would always be the same.

Levi had left the ranch, going on to have a wife and child. She had remained single and, it seemed, would never have a *familie* of her own.

Gott gives us what he wants us to have, she reminded herself, shamed by her uncharacteristic resentment of a woman she'd never met. A woman taken much too soon from her husband and son.

"I will pray you know happiness again, Levi."

A moment of silence stretched between them.

Levi opened his mouth, but he never had the chance to reply.

Chattering to herself, Florene rounded the barn. She held a wicker basket of garden clippings, and a billy goat trailed at her heels.

Spotting the trio, she raised a hand as if to wave. "I'm doing my chores," she grumbled, heading toward the rabbit pens.

A bell tinkling around its neck, the goat kicked up its heels when a playful puppy nipped at its fluffy tail.

"Hey, now! Leave Sassy alone." Florene shooed the pup away. "Gail, control your dogs, please."

Entranced by the miniature goat, Seth ran up. The puppy no longer held his interest. "Can I pet it?"

Florene shrugged. "Sure."

"It's so cute and soft," the boy enthused, running his hands gently over the goat's neck and back. "Does it follow you around all the time?"

"I suppose it does."

Gail found reason to smile. Watching Florene interact with her animals was always a pleasure. Though her younger sister had taken on a teenager's rebellious streak, deep down inside Florene was a kind and caring person. She had a way with four-legged creatures, and had successfully nursed many orphaned animals to maturity, even when they had no hope for survival.

After the goat's mother had rejected it, Florene had taken the lonesome baby to raise, bottle-feeding it around the clock until it was old enough to be weaned. Whenever she was outside, wherever Florene went, the goat went, too.

She unlatched the gate and stepped into the rabbit pen. "Come on, bunnies."

Snow-white save for their black-tipped ears and noses, the ruby-eyed rabbits hopped around, foraging through their morning breakfast, a selection of trimmings from the flower beds and gardens. The hares were voracious.

Since they were old enough, each girl had a specific chore that would teach the value of work. To earn her pin money, Florene sold her rabbits, chickens and eggs at the local farmers' market. She took great care choosing her breeding stock and selling the rest. She kept a few select rabbits and chickens as pets.

"Can I feed the bunnies?" Seth asked.

"If he's being a bother—" Levi started to say.

Basket empty, Florene shrugged again. "He can help with the chickens. I've got a lot of eggs to gather."

Wanting to speak with Levi alone, Gail said, "I need to go to town so I can clear up the business Mr. Slagel left undone." As much as she wanted to forget the whole sorry mess, the bank's threat loomed at the edge of her mind. "Levi," she continued, "would you give me a ride?"

Catching her hint, he nodded. "Sure. Can Florene keep an eye on Seth?"

Gail nodded. "Of course."

"I'll put the *boi* to work," Florene promised. "Can always use more hands."

Waiting until the two were out of earshot, Gail said, "Thank you for helping me."

"I'm honored you trust me," he said.

"I do. More than you know."

Sliding behind the wheel of his pickup, Levi reached for the ignition. "I think you've made the right decision," he said as he started the vehicle. The engine roared to life, humming smoothly. Having unhooked and set up the trailer, he no longer towed the heavy 5th wheel.

Gail climbed into the passenger's seat, with a manila folder in hand. It had taken her an additional hour to gather the paperwork she would require proving Slagel's theft. She still needed to go to the bank and get copies of the statements he'd concealed.

"I hate going to the police, but I don't think I have any other choice."

"If the man took that much money, you have to."

She clicked the seat belt into place and sighed. "The Lord says we are never to avenge ourselves."

"If I recall correctly, the Bible also says men shall be subject to the governing authorities. This is not vengeance, Gail. It is justice. This man's actions put your home and your living on the line. You might forgive him, but you also need to let the sheriff do his job."

Gail settled her hands calmly in her lap. "I know you're right. Even so, I can't help but wonder what would drive Mr. Slagel to steal from us. *Daed* always paid him fairly, as he did every man who worked here."

Putting the truck in gear, Levi guided it down the drive. "Some people are only honest until they find a way to take advantage. He probably wouldn't have tried it if your father were still alive."

Gail lowered her gaze. "I feel like such a fool."

Eyes going narrow, Levi sidled a look her way. "Stop blaming yourself. You are not responsible for that man's actions. You were unknowledgeable, and he took advantage of that."

"In other words, I am stupid."

Turning off the county road and onto the main highway that would take them into Burr Oak, Levi blew out a frustrated breath. "That's not what I said. If anyone is at fault, it is Samuel. He should have prepared you to take over, especially if his health was getting bad."

Her mouth went flat. "I am the one who failed him. *Daed* expected all of us to find suitable *ehmann*."

"You're what now—twenty-four?"

"*Ja.*"

"Surely you've had suitors. Don't tell me you didn't kiss a few boys during your *rumspringa*? At least one of them should have been worth marrying."

Gail's expression grew taut. "*Mamm* passed away when I came of age and there was so much to take care of. I never had a true *rumspringa*."

Levi gave himself a kick. If there had been a hole nearby, he'd have crawled into it.

As the oldest unmarried daughter, Gail would have naturally stepped up to take over the household. She also had three younger sisters to care for. Instead of running around and exploring life outside the Amish community—as well as having the chance to socialize with other *youngies* and find a potential mate—she was firmly and inextricably bound by her commitment and loyalty to her family.

"Well, you didn't miss much."

Giving him a knowing look, Gail cocked her head. "Does that shoe-leather taste good?"

"Delicious," he muttered under his breath.

She straightened her shoulders. "I have had a few beaus. Why, I could have married Albert Dekker last year if I'd had a mind to."

Levi dragged a hand over his mouth. "Albert Dekker," he repeated slowly. "Wasn't he the red-haired guy with the big ears who used to help deliver the hay?"

Gail bristled. "Albert's quite handsome now. He's proposed twice."

Levi sidled another look her way. "So why haven't you said yes?"

Temper flaring, Gail said, "Why are we even talking about my love life?" She struck the dash with a hand. "Can't you make this thing go faster? I believe my buggy could outrun this rattletrap."

Aware he'd hit a nerve, Levi backed off. It was one thing to josh around for fun, but quite another to hurt someone's feelings.

"We're getting there." To distract her, he turned on the radio to his favorite rock and roll station.

Arms crossed, Gail sat stiff, still stewing in her anger. "I like classical," she said, reaching out to switch the channel.

Remembering her mention of a cell phone, Levi said, "So, tell me what else had changed since I left."

A smile crept across her face, softening her serious expression and crinkling the corners of her eyes. "Many things," she said. "We might be Plain folks, but we're not the backward hicks some people still think we are."

Levi shook his head. "I never would have imagined your father would allow a cell phone and the like in the house."

"There is nothing in the Bible that says we can't have modern technology to make our lives more comfortable and our work less trying. It helps that Bishop Harrison is fair about what we may use and how. We live simple lives, but we are not stupid. Just—" she shrugged "—different."

"Nothing wrong with different."

"I suppose not." The questioning look returned to her gaze. "Do you regret leaving Amish life?"

Looking into her eyes, so clear and green as a field of clover, Levi felt an odd twist to his midsection. In the depths of her gaze was an openness that said she accepted all and would judge none. "Sometimes." He shrugged. "I mean, I thought I had the world figured out when I was younger."

"Did you?"

"Oh, not by a long shot." He chuckled, not in amusement but in wry regret. "In fact, in hindsight, I can say I knew nothing. Less than nothing. When I left the ranch, I was as shaky as a newborn colt."

"So that grass…was it greener in the *Englisch* world?"

"Let's just say I took a couple hard knocks. More than my share." His reply, a bit rueful, was also truthful. Life had not been easy or trouble free.

"So you haven't been entirely happy?"

Her question gave Levi pause. If he could go back and rewrite the pages of his life, he'd do some heavy editing. Other pages, he wished he could tear up and throw away.

"I'm happy I have Seth and that I'm healthy enough to earn us a living. Past that, I'm just grateful to be standing upright and going forward."

"Have you ever given thanks to *Gott* for keeping a hand over you and your *sohn*?" Gail asked quietly.

Levi had no reply. Nevertheless, her question gave him food for thought. Perhaps the belief that he'd gotten himself through the tough times wasn't entirely accurate.

"Maybe I should," he said, not sure he was ready to commit one way or another. He'd sat in church long enough to have a good knowledge of the Bible, though years had passed since he'd been compelled to crack one open.

Gail, on the other hand, had no qualms about seeking divine guidance. Before making a decision, she'd sat down at the table in front of her father's old Bible and prayed for *Gott* to give her the wisdom she needed. Obedience to the church was a cornerstone of the Amish faith.

Despite his cynicism, Levi had to wonder if his own life would have been a little easier if he'd laid his burdens at the feet of the Lord?

The thought, fleeting as it was, burrowed into his mind.

More miles disappeared beneath the rolling wheels of his pickup. Passing over a low rise, the town came into view.

"Recognize it?" Gail asked.

Levi glanced around, looking for familiar landmarks. Even though he sometimes passed by when following the rodeo circuit through Texas, he'd never stopped long enough to take in all the changes to his hometown.

"So much has changed. It seems…bigger."

With exactly ten blocks and nary a stoplight in sight, the community grew up around a group of Old Order Amish families branching out from Pennsylvania in the 1930s. Seeking to take advantage of cheap and plentiful land, the settlers found the northern part of the state perfect for farming and ranching.

Through the years the population had expanded, as had the need for more public amenities. A courthouse and a post office had been established, as was an independent school district and a public library. Newer additions included a shining new stop-n-go convenience store with a row of gas pumps and a dollar store.

A sense of nostalgia tugged at his heartstrings. Driving through his hometown resurrected many of the good times he'd experienced when living with the Schroder family. What he'd once viewed as a boring and mundane were now cherished memories.

Shaking off his thoughts, Levi glanced toward Gail. Going silent, she stared out the window. Face pinched with worry, her mouth curved down, Walter Slagel's betrayal had clearly taken a toll on her.

Though he wanted to comfort her, Levi resisted the urge to reach for her hand. It wouldn't be proper to display such familiarity.

That she turned to him in her time of need had roused his protective instincts. He'd promised to help her untangle this mess, and he intended to follow through.

"Everything's going to be all right," he said attempting to lighten her mood.

She forced a smile. "I pray you are right."

"We'll figure this out," he returned, injecting confidence into his voice. "You have my word."

Chapter Five

Sheriff Evan Miller slid the paperwork across the desk toward Gail. "Please sign here."

Stomach knotted with anxiety, Gail looked over the typed documents the lawman had prepared. Hesitating, she didn't reach for the pen Miller offered. "What happens when I do?"

Miller leaned back in his chair. "Well, we'll take the complaint to the judge. Once he determines a crime has been committed, he will issue an arrest warrant. After that happens, we'll keep an eye out for Slagel."

"And then?"

"When he's arrested, the DA will file charges and it will go to court," Miller said. "Given the evidence against him, he'll probably get some lengthy prison time."

Looking at her old school friend Gail hesitated. While she had only gone to the eighth grade, Evan Miller had left the Amish and followed a career in law enforcement.

"I've never put a man in jail before."

"We can't do anything if you won't sign these," the

lawman prodded. "It's entirely your decision, of course, but I would say you'd be making a grave mistake if you decide to let him walk."

"You have to do it, Gail," Levi said softly. "If he's stolen from you, he'll steal from others."

She nodded. Knowing the Amish were reluctant to involve the law when they were victims of crime was probably why Walter Slagel believed he could walk away unscathed.

"I understand your hesitations," Evan Miller continued. "On one hand, you were raised to be forgiving of trespasses. On the other hand, Mr. Slagel didn't take just a few hundred dollars, which would be a petty misdemeanor. However, what he did was commit first-degree felony theft. Under Texas law, that adds up to a long stretch in prison."

"Is there no way to catch him and just make him repay the money? Then we wouldn't have to press charges."

Evan Miller shook his head. "It doesn't quite work that way. We can't put out an arrest warrant unless you sign—" he tapped the pages with his index finger "—these papers so we can file charges. No complaint, Slagel walks. Simple as that."

The invisible weight on her shoulders pressed harder. Her family had worked hard through many generations to build Schroder Ranch into one of the most highly sought Amish suppliers of prime organic meat. Schroder Longhorns were not just cattle; they were lovingly bred with an eye toward excellence.

Losing the money brought operations to a halt. True, she still had the land, equipment and cattle. But all that was now heavily mortgaged to the bank. And without cash to pay the vendors who supplied the machinery, feeds and other necessary items to run the operations, and cover payroll, Schroder Ranch was, effectively, spinning its wheels.

Stupid. Stupid. Stupid.

The word echoed repeatedly in Gail's mind.

If only she had been born a man instead of a woman, her father would have taught her the skills it took to run the ranch. Because she was a woman, all she was allowed to learn was cooking, cleaning and tending *kinder*.

Her mind flitted back to an earlier thought. If there was a way out of this disaster, she intended to learn how to run the ranch on her own. Not only the books, but everything about the cattle. Knowing Levi wouldn't be staying long, she must be prepared to stand on her own two feet.

Many an Amish widow had stepped into the business their husbands had established. Moreover, more and more single Amish women were branching out into business, running farm stands or small retail shops of their own, like her sister Amity.

Why couldn't she do the same? A daughter couldn't carry on her father's name, but she could certainly keep the Schroder legacy alive.

Things are going to change, starting today.

Expression going hard, she reached for the pen. Writing in her careful script, she signed the papers. She pushed them back across the desk and gave the sheriff a direct look. "I'll pray for Mr. Slagel's salvation. Until then, the law needs to deal with him here on earth."

Sheriff Miller collected his paperwork. "And that we will do." Standing, he came around his desk to shake hands with her and Levi, and escort them out. "I'll be in touch."

Gail nodded. "I hope we hear from you soon."

Levi accepted the sheriff's gesture. "Thank you for all you've done. We appreciate your time."

"I'll head over to see the judge as soon as I can," Miller promised. "Once he puts this in motion, we can put out an arrest warrant for Slagel. Hopefully, the information Gail provided will aid us in tracking him down. People usually run back to the places that are familiar, and knowing he has contacts in Oklahoma will help a lot."

"I know you'll do your best."

He offered a smile. "It's good to see you, Gail."

Gail touched the sheriff's arm. "You, too, Evan. And thank you for helping us through this."

Task complete, she departed the sheriff's office, stepping out into the afternoon sun. Levi fell into step beside her.

"I'm proud of you. That was brave of you to do."

Gail swallowed thickly. "I should have been wiser, more discerning. Instead, I let my own ignorance blind me."

"You were in mourning," Levi said gently. "This Slagel—for one reason or another, he saw an opportunity and took it."

"If he had troubles, all he had to do was ask for help. We would have given him anything he needed." She looked at him. "I know the Lord commands us to be forgiving, but I'm struggling with that."

"It's only right that you feel betrayed," Levi returned gently. "That's part of life. It might take time, but those feelings will pass."

Gail closed her eyes, and then opened and rubbed them. Her nights had been sleepless ones since Slagel disappeared. Allowing anger and disappointment get the better of her would only drag her down into despair.

"I hope so."

"Slagel dealt you a blow, but you don't have to let it beat you," he continued. "You've got resources."

She nodded. "It's been difficult for me to realize that because I felt like I was gazing down a dark hole with no end in sight. Now, I see I had it wrong the entire time. I need to look up, toward the Lord and the light of His grace and guidance. There will be a way to overcome this. I have to have faith."

Levi offered a smile of encouragement. "Amen to that."

Levi glanced around as he and Gail headed back toward the lot where he'd parked his pickup.

The downtown area was a pleasant one. Trees and neatly clipped hedges bordered part of the town's center, reserved as a rest area. Shaded benches and a gazebo overlooked a stone fountain and walkway fashioned out of natural stone.

The town impressed visitors with the quaint, old-fashioned ambience that harkened back to a gentler era. Small businesses prospered along the main street, a mix of Amish and *Englisch* that blended together in harmony. Just as they were about to cross the street, a man dressed in a short-sleeved white shirt, coveralls and boots jogged up. "Gail? Gail Schroder?"

Stopping mid-step, Gail turned. "What can I do for you, Mr. Yost?"

Levi recognized the owner of the local feedstore,

Linus Yost. No longer a rail-thin teenager, Linus had grown into a bear of a man with muscles developed from years of hefting sacks of heavy feed and massive bales of hay.

Pushing back his straw hat, Yost offered an apologetic smile. "I hate to bother you, Miss Schroder, but your account at the store is overdue and hasn't been paid in months."

Gail pasted on a smile. "I apologize for making you wait for your money," she said. "Mr. Slagel has left, and I've been trying to hire a new manager."

"I understand things slip through the cracks, and that you've got your hands full, what with your *daed*'s passing and all. But I have got a business to run, and if people do not pay their bills, I can't stay open."

"I understand completely. I—just—"

Levi stepped forward. "I'll be in to pay the bill this afternoon."

Linus Yost scratched beneath his lower lip. His beard indicated him to be a married man. "Levi?" he said behind a squint. "I didn't recognize you there for a minute." He offered his hand. "You sure have changed."

Levi accepted his gesture. "Nice to see you, too, Linus."

"I had no word you'd come back."

"Thought I'd stop by and stay a few days and catch up."

"Didn't know you were still in touch with anyone around here," Linus said.

"I let a lot of water go under the bridge, but I'm trying to make up for that."

"We're all very glad Levi has come home," Gail added. "Truth be told, I need the help."

Linus beamed. "Well, I'm glad to hear that, too. Your *daed* always said he was the best hand that ever worked cattle on his ranch."

"I don't disagree," Gail said.

"I have to get back to work." Tipping his hat, Linus offered his hand again. "Come in any time."

Levi waved a hand. "I'll be in to settle that bill."

After the man was out of earshot, Gail tossed him a look. "Levi, you're not responsible for our bills."

"The animals still have to eat and you're going to need supplies to keep them fed." He shrugged. "I've got a little money tucked away, so it's not a problem. I will pay the bill." To make her feel less beholden, he added, "You can pay me back when you've sorted through this mess. Until then, let me take care of things."

"I—I don't know what to say." Gail's eyes looked like they were starting to well up with tears.

Not comfortable with any shows of emotion at that moment, he rummaged for his keys, then glanced across the street. A small café beckoned.

His brow crinkled. Years ago, the space had been an empty lot. Now a business flourished there.

"Come on," he said, checking his watch. The morning, so full of activity, had given way to late afternoon. Lunch had come and gone, and his energy was beginning to wane. A good jolt of caffeine would give him a much-needed boost. Gail, too, could probably use a chance to sit down and rest.

"I'd like a cup of coffee. How about you?"

"A cup of tea would be wonderful about now." Acquiescing, Gail allowed him to lead the way.

Levi pushed open the front door, and they walked into a small but cheery dining area. Composed of an eclectic mix of brick, wood and other stone, the decor had a sweet, old-fashioned ambience.

Though the lunch run had apparently ended, the café buzzed with activity. Patrons talked and laughed, attended by waitresses.

A variety of tantalizing aromas wafted from the kitchen. From the day's specials listed on a blackboard on the wall, he could see the café served a mix of traditional Amish and *Englisch* foods. It seemed to be a popular spot for locals and tourists alike.

A slender young woman in a neat dress and apron was ready to help. Her blond hair was tucked under her white *kapp*, and her bright eyes sparkled with welcome. The pin she wore identified her as Alma.

"Guten nachmittag," she greeted as she guided them to a booth.

"Thank you," Levi said after they'd sat down. "Could I get some coffee—and bring whatever the lady would like."

"Hot tea," Gail said. "With honey and lemon."

A moment later Alma returned with their beverages. "Please let me know when you're ready to order." She left two menus on the table.

Levi took a sip of the hot brew. "That hits the spot."

Dunking her tea bag into the hot water, Gail looked around. "Been a long time since I've sat in a café. *Mamm* always said why eat out when we've got food at home."

He lowered his cup. "True. But sometimes a person needs to get out and enjoy themselves a little, just to socialize. How long has it been since you've been out?"

"Why, I go out fairly often," Gail said in her own defense.

"Where?"

She thought a moment. "Well, I go to church. There's always a potluck, and a singalong or other games."

"Yeah, but those are mostly for the kids," he said. "What do you do to relax, cut loose?"

"A couple of times a month I go to the library. And there's always a quilting bee going on."

Levi rolled his eyes. "None of that really sounds like fun."

Gail bristled, giving him a narrow look. "It is fun to me."

Levi was about to respond when the door of the café opened. A couple of rough-looking men shuffled inside. Their conversation was loud and coarse.

Catching sight of him, one of the men raised a hand in greeting. "There you are," he called.

Levi waved back in a half-hearted manner. These men were part of the same rodeo circuit and they often traveled in a group from event to event. Before leaving Montana, they had all agreed to meet up in Burr Oak, but he'd gotten sidetracked.

The men, Bill Reece and his brother, Shane, ambled up.

"Levi," Bill greeted. "Thought we'd lost you and Seth."

"Got tired and pulled over," Levi said, offering no further explanation. Cowboys were worse than women when it came to gossiping and he liked to keep his business to himself.

"Looks to me like you ditched us for some female company," Shane observed, and winked.

Levi bristled at the assumption. Bill and Shane Reece were single and ran with the partying crowd, one that he'd definitely had to step away from after becoming a parent.

"It's not that way at all," he said, immediately correcting the notion. "I just stopped to visit friends."

"Oh?" Bill released a snort of disbelief. "And who might this lady here be?"

Wanting the men to move along, Levi hurried through the introductions. "Gail Schroder, this is Bill and Shane Reece."

Both removed their hats.

"Nice to meet you," Bill Reece said.

"Sorry to interrupt," his younger brother added.

Clearly uncomfortable with their comments, Gail nodded politely. "Gentlemen."

"Gail is Amish, so mind your manners," Levi warned, making his displeasure clear. "Please, remember you are in the presence of a lady."

"Of course," Bill Reece said, and looked to Levi. "You ready for this weekend?"

Levi waved a hand to interrupt. "Gail hasn't got any interest in the rodeo or in bronc riding, fellas," he said and shot them both a look. "We'd like to get back to our conversation, if you don't mind."

Much to his relief, both men took the hint to move on.

"We'll catch up later," Bill said.

Shane tipped his head. "See you around."

"Maybe," Levi countered, offering no firm commitment.

The cowboys walked off, taking a booth at the opposite end of the café.

Suddenly self-conscious, Levi turned to Gail. "Sorry

about that. I didn't know they were going to show up. They can be a little uncouth, if you know what I mean."

"It's not a problem," she allowed graciously. "I enjoyed meeting your friends."

"Not really my friends," he corrected. "Just some guys I know from the rodeo circuit."

"I see." She pursed her lips. "I hope I'm not keeping you from anything important."

"I'd rather visit with you than hang out with those fellas," he insisted.

"I appreciate that, Levi." Pushing her tea aside, Gail slid out of the booth. "Would you mind if we go? I feel I should be home. There's so much work to do, and we have no hands."

"Of course." Standing, Levi took out his wallet and dug out a five-dollar bill, which he left on the table to cover their drinks and the tip.

They strolled toward the exit.

"I'd still like to post a help-wanted notice in the local newspaper," she said. "Would you mind driving me there?"

"Not at all." Pausing to open the door for her, he added. "Sorry I was teasing you before Bill and Shane interrupted. I didn't mean to make you angry."

"I'm not angry, Levi. You gave me something to think about." Her expression grew pensive. "I think you are right. I do need to get out more. Once we have straightened out things with the bank, I might get out and kick up my heels, so to speak."

He exhaled, relieved she wasn't upset. "I'm glad to hear that."

Gail offered a smile. "Thank you for all you've done.

I wouldn't have gotten through this morning without your help."

"I'll do what I can," he promised.

Escorting her outside, Levi considered the task ahead. It would take a lot of effort to put the Schroder ranch back into the black, but he had no doubt about Gail's determination to save her family's homestead.

Holding up his own plans a week or two to help her sort through the mess Slagel had left behind wouldn't cost him more than a little time. His schedule wasn't carved in stone.

Truth be told, now that he and Gail had reconnected, he was looking forward to spending time with her.

Staying on to lend a hand gave him the perfect excuse.

Chapter Six

The evening was subdued as Gail and her sisters gathered in the living room after a light supper. Because the entire day had been chaotic, she'd rushed to put something to eat on the table. After the meal, everyone settled into their favorite chairs. Never ones to let their hands be idle, each had some ongoing needlework project they worked on.

Levi sat among them, quietly sipping his coffee. He'd promised to say nothing about the bank agent's visit, and he kept his word. Given some paper and colored pencils, Seth stretched out on the thick, handwoven rug in front of the black-grated fireplace. Within minutes, he was asleep. The puppy he'd commandeered earlier in the day lay contentedly nearby, basking in the warm glow.

Gail knew Levi didn't approve of lying to her sisters about the state of their finances, but from her point of view it wasn't exactly a deception at all. More like a delay. She'd wanted to explore all her options before settling on a course of action. The news she had to deliver would be upsetting enough. Being able to present a solution would help allay the trauma.

Lowering her needlework, she cleared her throat. "I have something I need to say," she began slowly.

"It has to do with why that man was here earlier, doesn't it?" Rebecca asked presciently.

"I knew something was wrong," Amity added.

Florene barely glanced up. Her attention was tied to her smartphone.

"There's no easy way to say this, so I will just spit it out. The reason Walter Slagel ran off is because he stole the money from the last sale of cattle we sent to auction."

Rebecca's mouth folded into a frown. "I didn't have a good feeling about that man. No one honest packs up and leaves in the middle of the night."

"How much did he embezzle?" Amity asked, surprisingly calm.

"All of it," Gail said. "I've filed a report with the police, and now we wait for the law to do its work."

Sorting through swatches, Rebecca pushed her glasses back up on her nose. "Will the money Slagel took be recoverable?"

Levi glanced up. "Cash rarely is."

"The news doesn't get better. The loan *Daed* took out hasn't been paid for months." Reaching in her apron pocket, Gail produced the paperwork outlining the foreclosure threat. "Unfortunately, he mortgaged the homestead. The bank intends to take it in a month's time."

Florene finally glanced up from her smartphone. "So we're going to be homeless. Fantastic." Her voice smacked of sarcasm. "Great job."

Stung by her words, Gail felt her insides clench. "I

did the best I could," she said in her own defense. "I had no reason not to trust Mr. Slagel."

"When *Daed* was alive, he always kept a close eye on him," Rebecca chimed in. "Nothing got past him."

"Slagel clearly saw the opportunity after *Daed*'s passing and took it," Amity pointed out. "That shows a devious mind at work.

"He sold the cattle as his own," Gail confirmed. "And kept the money. The check and bill of sale he showed me was fake."

Amity nodded knowingly. "With a computer and a few clicks of a mouse, you can make anything look real nowadays."

Rebecca's lips thinned. "I understand technology can be a useful tool. But I'm glad the bishop bans us from having computers in our homes." Turning her head, she shot a look of disapproval at Florene.

Catching her sister's insinuation, Florene turned her cell phone facedown. "I don't think texting with my friends is wrong," she countered. "Besides, I'm not baptized, and I'm not staying Amish." Crossing her arms in front of her, she gave them a defiant look.

Unruffled by her younger sister's outburst, Gail didn't blink an eye. "That's fine." Needing something to do with her hands, she picked up her mending and nipped the thread to break the connection from the needle. "When are you moving?"

"What?" Caught by surprise, Florene stammered. "M-moving?"

Gail calmly continued. "As in packing your bags and leaving."

"Well…n…not until I'm eighteen," Florene answered, looking flustered.

"That's still a year away," Gail countered. "So, while you are still living under this roof, you will live by the rules of this house. And as the bishop said, cell phones are only for emergencies. Spending hours texting or on social media is not life-or-death."

Florene's expression darkened. "That's not fair! It's my right during my *rumspringa*."

Ever the peacemaker, Amity waved her hands. "Hold up," she said, calling for a time-out. "We're letting petty things distract us from more important issues." Turning to her younger sister, she put out a single finger. "It's true you're not baptized, but you are still part of an Amish family and were raised to be courteous to your elders. Have enough respect to put your phone aside when you are with family. Take it elsewhere if you want to message your friends."

Florene pouted as she turned off her phone and slid it into the pocket of her apron.

Amity then turned to Gail. "Now for you."

Gail's brows shot high. "Me?"

Amity pierced her with a frown. "*Ja*, you. For months you've been acting like life is a great burden."

"We've all tried to help you, but you've pushed us away, insisting you could handle things here on the ranch," Rebecca chimed in. "Well, I have news for you. You can't do it all, and now we're in a fine mess."

"But—" Tossing her mending back into the basket at her feet, Gail threw up her hands in frustration. "There's so much to do! How do I handle an entire ranch?"

"Learn!" Amity snapped.

"I intend to," Gail said, speaking more calmly than she felt. "I've talked to Levi and there is a solution."

Amity crossed her arms. "We're all listening."

"What are you going to do?" Rebecca asked.

Gail nodded to Levi. He'd been quiet throughout the entire exchange. "Please, explain."

Setting aside his coffee, Levi stood up. "Cattle aren't called *money on the hoof* for nothing. The best thing to do is cull some cattle from the herd and take them to auction. That will put money back in the bank. You won't get top dollar, but it should be enough to carry you through until the spring calves are ready for sale in the fall."

"How long will that take?" Amity asked.

"I'll need a little time to go through the herd and make my choices," Levi said. "You'll want to keep the cows that are of breeding age and cut those that haven't rebred on schedule. If they are not expecting or haven't got a spring calf by their side, they'll be on the chopping block."

"I wouldn't have known what to do," Gail admitted. "Levi is the one guiding me. Even though he has commitments of his own, he's agreed to stay and help us get the cattle to auction." She paused and then added, "He's also been generous enough to loan us a little money. Some bills were also unpaid, and he's been kind enough to cover them."

"Thank *Gott* you came, Levi," Rebecca said.

"I owe your family a debt of gratitude and I intend to repay it," Levi said softly. "I promised Gail I'd help out, and I will."

Amazed, Gail felt her heart fill with hope. The bank agent's dire warning was no longer a threat, but a challenge to be overcome. As she was the eldest of the sisters, keeping the family together, both physically and spiritually, would fall on her shoulders.

"I think now would be a good time to have a Bible study," she said quietly. "It will be a good reminder that *Gott* is always with us, even through difficult times."

"I heartily agree," Rebecca said. Laying aside her project, she reached for the Bible on the end table. Opening the pages, she read from a passage. "See here in Matthew: The rain came down, the streams rose, and the winds blew and beat against that house; yet it did not fall."

"A house divided will," Amity added with some emphasis. "We must remember not to claw at each other's eyes like angry cats."

"*Daed* would be so disappointed in us," Rebecca added.

"*Mamm*, too, wouldn't want to see us talking down to each other," Amity added. "I think we should all make the promise that from now on, we will think before we speak in anger."

"That would be nice," Florene said after a moment. "If it means anything, I'll try harder not to aggravate you all with my cell phone."

"Well, that's a good start," Rebecca said drily.

Looking at her younger siblings, Gail felt her heart overflow with gratitude. Despite their quibbling, she loved them with all her heart. No matter what happened, they would always be sisters. And as sisters, they would always stick together no matter what might happen in their lives.

Her gaze turned to Levi.

The teenage boy she remembered had grown into a man. When she'd panicked over the banker's visit, he'd

kept his wits, analyzing the situation and finding a solution that would keep the property out of foreclosure.

I am so blessed to have my family, she thought.

And that included Levi.

Stretched out in his bunk in the RV, Levi found rest
eluded him. He desperately needed sleep, but every time
he shut his eyes, they popped right back open. He was
too keyed up.

Myriad details rustled through his head like the cattle he'd be tending. The Longhorns were the backbone
of the entire operation. Without those cows, the ranch
wouldn't be viable or profitable. Though he'd been away
for over a decade, it was easy to recall most everything
he'd learned as a young cowhand. *It was only a couple
of weeks,* he reminded himself. *And then they'd be rolling down the road, on their way.*

But the idea of leaving didn't seem so enticing. Restless, Levi swung his legs over the edge of his bunk and
stood up. Taking care not to disturb Seth, he slipped
into the adjoining bathroom and shut the door. Splash-
ing hot water on his face to revive his flagging energy,
he stared into the mirror above the narrow vanity. The
reflection of a tired man stared back.

Having spent most of his working career on the road,
he had to admit that he was getting worn down from the
constant travel from state to state. He and Seth rarely
stayed in one town more than a few weeks.

When he was single, he'd enjoyed living a nomadic
lifestyle. Marrying Betheny had settled him somewhat,
but it was not destined to last.

Now that he was a father, the needs of his child
preyed on his mind. Seth was growing like a weed.

Every time he parked the RV, the trailer felt smaller and more cramped. Soon the day would come when the two of them would need a more permanent living arrangement. And Seth was almost old enough to start first grade, but the child could barely read or write. Despite that, Seth was a smart kid. Given a chance, he'd probably excel in school. He deserved a stable home and a decent education.

"It's getting time to do something else," Levi muttered to himself.

But what?

Having competed in the rodeo most of his adult life, he had limited experience in the working world. Not many people had a use for men who rode wild horses. Nearing thirty, his youth was fading. Time would soon become an enemy. Eventually, he'd have to walk away from the sport. A man could only take so much wear and tear before the mileage started to register on his body.

Hanging up his towel, he sighed. Going *Englisch* had expanded his knowledge about the world, but the fact remained that he still only had an eighth-grade education. There were not many employment options for a man of his age or experience.

Knowing he'd have to make some hard decisions soon, he cracked the door to check on Seth. The child slept in his own small bunk, surrounded by a multitude of toys. But not all the animals were inanimate. The pup Seth had set his cap on had somehow found its way into the RV. Already, a mat with a food and water dish sat out in the tiny kitchenette, along with some newspapers for accidents. Snuggled in the boy's embrace, the mongrel had made itself quite at home. By the looks of it, it was not going to be a small dog, either.

Levi shook his head. Of course, the kid had gotten his way.

His gaze shifted, taking in more details. A picture frame welded to the wall and decorated with the word "Mommy" hung above Seth's head. A nightlight was nearby, illuminating the image of Seth's mother. Seth believed his mother watched over him from heaven, so he always wanted the light on so she could see him. In the child's mind, it made sense.

If only Seth knew Betheny didn't want him...

Chest going tight, Levi crept to the front of the RV. Thinking about the past would do no good. He could never undo or rewrite what had happened.

Filling the coffee maker with water, he added a scoop of pure Colombian roast to the basket. There was nothing better than a good strong cup of coffee to clear a man's head.

Pouring himself a cup a few minutes later, he sat down at the table. Around him, the kitchen and living room blended into a single living space, separated by a counter serving double duty as a breakfast bar. Down a short hall was the bathroom and a bedroom with two bunks and other storage spaces.

There had been no reason to hang on to the house he and Betheny had bought on the outskirts of Reno, Nevada. Sitting on a few acres of land, the house was picture perfect with its white picket fence and large fenced-in yard. All the hopes and dreams he'd had for his wife and child had gone up in smoke.

He pushed the thoughts away, refusing to think about

all the mistakes he'd made. It was better to leave that past behind and walk away.

Sipping his coffee, Levi glanced out the window. After unhitching the trailer, he'd parked it just opposite the barn. Despite the thick line of trees bracketing the main house, he had a clear view of it through the backyard.

Looking at the place he'd briefly called home, he thought about all that had happened since he'd pulled into the drive. Samuel and Sarah Schroder were gone now, and Gail was the head of the house. A blind man could see she was struggling. She'd never been taught how to deal with the cattle. As a daughter, it was not her place to work out on the range.

Levi had to wonder what might have happened had he stayed in Burr Oak and gotten baptized. More than once, Samuel Schroder had hinted that he'd be willing to have him join the family as a son-in-law. Surely, out of his four daughters, Levi might find one of the girls to be a suitable bride.

Remembering how he'd brushed Samuel off, Levi frowned. Though it was common for the Amish to be married and starting their own families at a young age, his attention had always been fixed on his own ambitions.

Ambitions that didn't include getting married.

At least, not right away. There was a big world outside of Burr Oak, Texas, and he'd wanted to see it. Back then, he'd never paid any girl any attention. Certainly not Gail. All willowy limbs and pigtails, she was about eleven when her parents had taken him in. One thing he remembered most about her was her inability to keep herself tidy. Her white *kapp* was always askew, her braids always unwinding. Wearing her heart on her sleeve, she'd trailed him like a lovesick calf.

But he never gave her a second look. Having discovered the world of cowboying, he'd gotten pulled into the excitement of the rodeos. From his point of view, horses were far more interesting than gawky little girls.

Ashamed of how he'd treated her, Levi frowned. Had he hung around the ranch long enough for her to mature, there was no doubt in his mind he'd have sat up and taken notice.

What a fool.

Viewing her in a whole new light, he shook his head. Running off, he'd blown it. No doubt there. He couldn't court Gail now even if he wanted to. They walked in two different worlds.

Setting aside his empty cup, Levi felt a sense of longing settle deep inside his chest. He'd been raised by people who were models of self-sufficiency. Most of their food came from the garden and meat was plentiful enough. Chickens and rabbits were regularly served, along with beef, pork and lamb. Working from sunup to sundown, the Amish only purchased what they couldn't make or grow themselves. As for clothes, most everything he'd worn as a kid was handmade. The biggest treat of the year was a new pair of boots at Christmas. Everything else was made with love.

Faith. Home. Family. It all sounded so good.

Swallowing against the lump building at the back of his throat, Levi blinked hard. He wanted that again.

He just wasn't sure how to go about getting it. He'd always chosen the wrong path and burned the wrong bridges, a flaw he needed to work on if he ever hoped to achieve any sort of stability for himself and his son.

Chapter Seven

By the time her busy day ended, Gail wanted nothing more than to collapse on her bed. All the stress and activity the day had piled on her psyche made the space behind her temples thud. She'd been going nonstop since early morning. Dropping into bed at the scandalously late hour of 10:00 p.m., all she wanted to do was close her eyes.

Sleep, however, eluded her.

Tossing and turning, Gail struggled to find a comfortable spot on the bed. Another long night stretched ahead. Constant worry over her many responsibilities had worn her down to a nub. Exhaustion dogged her every waking moment.

For months, she'd been unable to find solace in her prayers, feeling every bit like a pilgrim lost in the wilderness. Levi's unexpected return had given her a sign *Gott* had heard her plea.

Rolling over onto her side, Gail attempted to regulate her breathing. Her mind kept racing, going off in wild directions. All the emotions she'd believed extinguished had come down on her like a ton of rocks. Banked embers of feelings had reignited.

Levi was home.

It was almost too good to be true.

Her thoughts drifted back to a time when she was younger and still innocent. Of course, she'd had a crush on him as big as the state of Texas, practically since the first day her parents had announced they would take in the orphaned boy. From the moment she'd laid eyes on him, she trailed him like a puppy, wishing he'd look her way.

Alas, he never looked at her twice.

As it inevitably did, time had unwound itself, disappearing into the ether. One year rolled into another, and then a decade had passed in the blink of an eye. She and Levi had changed: strangers becoming friends who'd again become strangers when he'd chosen to pursue the ambition that would take him far away from the prairie and lakes region surrounding Burr Oak, Texas.

Suddenly, she sat up, pressing a hand to her chest. "Dear *Gott*, help me stop thinking about Levi."

Knowing sleep would be elusive for her, she pushed aside the heavy covers, swung her legs over the edge of the bed and turned on her bedside lamp. She rubbed her eyes and glanced around the familiar space.

Like most Plain people, she preferred her private space to be neat and simple. Though the smallest, her room was the most comfortable, filled with a half bed and side table, an armoire, a rocking chair, and a shelf for personal items. A vanity with a deep porcelain basin and matching pitcher occupied one corner. Most every piece of furniture in the old house was an antique, hand-crafted by Amish carpenters. The quilt on her bed was handmade, stitched before she was born.

A squat, flat-top iron stove also sat in one corner of the room. As the rambling old farmhouse didn't have central heating, the stove was very much in use during the cold season. Not only did it provide much-needed heat to the upper floor, but it was also a convenient way to make a quick cup of tea or heat water when she wanted water to wash her face. During the winter, the fire inside its black belly crackled, radiating with a reassuring warmth.

Pouring water from the pitcher into the vanity basin, she splashed her face before combing out her hair. She wove the thick, unruly mass into a tight bun. As usual, a few stubborn tendrils escaped, framing her face with stray curls.

Avoiding her usual drab choice, she chose a fresh dress sewn in peacock green. It was one usually reserved for socializing, but rarely worn. As an unmarried woman she could wear brighter colors, as a signal to men that she was single. Might as well get some use out of it instead of letting it rot on the hanger, unused. She slipped on the dress and tied a clean white apron around her waist. Last was her *kapp*, pinned into place.

Though the hours of night had begun to pass away, it was still too early to go downstairs.

Pulling up a chair, Gail set down and opened her Bible. A few hours of prayer and meditation on the coming day ahead would help clear her mind. Months had passed since she had spent quiet time, giving praise and thanks to *Gott* for his wisdom and the many mercies he'd granted her family through the generations.

By time the sun began to peek over the far horizon,

several hours had passed since she sat down to read. For her study, she'd chosen to revisit the story of Job. Job had lost everything, but he'd never given up his faith, and for that the Lord had blessed him twofold.

Feeling humbled and inspired, Gail put her Bible away.

I give my burden to you, Lord. Please bless the day ahead.

Humming under her breath, she went downstairs. Time was getting away and there was a lot of work ahead. After coaxing the old cookstove back to life with a bellyful of wood and lots of kindling, she set to putting together breakfast. She had two extra people to cook for now.

One by one, her sisters filtered downstairs to tend to their morning chores before breakfast. Eggs would be gathered, the cows milked, and other sundry tasks would be taken care of before anyone ate a single bite.

As a surprise, Gail made bread pudding. Mixing a bowl of fresh eggs, milk, diced apples, raisins, cinnamon, sugar and a touch of nutmeg, she poured the mixture over leftover bread from yesterday's baking, and then sprinkled over a generous helping of pecans. She slid the pan into the oven and then whipped up a vanilla sauce to drizzle on top.

She put on a pot of freshly ground coffee to brew, and then set to frying up several thick slabs of ham. She prepared double the amount, planning to make sandwiches for lunch. But sandwiches were not any good without fresh bread, prompting her to prepare a loaf of sourdough to go into the oven. Within half an hour, it filled the kitchen with a scrumptious aroma.

Drawn by the amazing scents filling the air, her sisters gathered back in the kitchen, ready for the morning meal. Florene had brought in plenty of eggs and Rebecca had a bucket of fresh milk. Later, the milk would be churned into butter, and the leavings would become fresh buttermilk.

Dunking a tea bag into a mug, Rebecca blinked. "My gosh, I haven't seen you in that dress in ages, Gail. You hardly ever wear it."

More interested in food than fashion, Amity hovered near the stove. "Something smells wonderful."

"Bread pudding." Gail slid a pair of mitts onto her hands and opened the oven to retrieve the pan. The pudding had set, perfectly browned. She placed it on the counter to cool.

Amity bent over the pan. "You rarely make this."

"I know why," Rebecca said behind a knowing grin. "It is Levi's favorite, and we all know the way to a man's heart is through his stomach."

Amity rolled her eyes. "*Ach*, now I remember the torch you carried for that boy."

Cheeks going hot, Gail dipped her head. When they were younger, her sisters had teased her unmercifully over her infatuation for Levi. It didn't help that one of them had found a page that once dropped from her school notebook, the one on which she'd written "Mrs. Levi Wyse" and "Gail Wyse" in her neat, angular schoolgirl script.

"That was ages ago. I was just a child," she countered. "We all had our silly moments then."

"If he asked you now, I bet you would marry him," Florene teased.

"Oh, don't be foolish!" Gail exclaimed.

Florene's smile dropped. "Take a chill pill," she

tossed back at her, sliding into the slang she picked up from her *Englisch* friends.

Rebecca's gaze rose sharply. As a teacher, she rarely countenanced inappropriate behavior, and would quickly call out the offender with a stern warning. She often acted as the peacemaker in the family. "Hold on now," she said, stepping between the two sisters. "There's no reason to get snappy with each other."

Florene dropped into her chair. "Can't have a bit of fun around here," she grumbled.

Rebecca waggled a warning finger. "Don't, Florene." Whirling on her heel, she went after Gail. "And where did your ugly temper come from?"

Gail angled her chin. "I don't like being teased." Fuming, she turned back to her cooking, cracking eggs into a bowl. Fork in hand, she whipped them into a froth.

"Florene was just funning you," Amity added, anxiously playing the peacemaker. "We've all had our infatuations. Doesn't mean we're in love."

"Gail's not married because no man wants a mean old spinster," Florene stated, sticking out her tongue.

Gail was stung by the insult. Her throat suddenly closed, blocking her air. "Someone finish the cooking, please."

She set aside the frothed eggs. Blinking back tears, she hurried out the back door. The argument had entirely ruined her mood. Though she knew her youngest sister was just being a brat, the fact she was still unmarried and childless bothered her more than she cared to admit.

Hardly paying attention to where she was going, she plowed straight into Levi. His straw hat went flying.

"Oh!" Her voice squeaked with surprise and her heart slammed against her chest. As she attempted to get out of his way, her heel snagged on a paving stone lining the walkway. Arms pinwheeling, she landed in a heap.

"Are you all right?"

Dazed, Gail pressed a hand to her forehead. What a way to start the day, flat on her backside.

Embarrassment heated her cheeks. She wasn't sure if she should laugh or cry. Her breath caught in a hitch. "I—I'm fine."

Levi leaned down, reaching out to her. Slowly, he helped her get to her feet. "I'm such an oaf," he said by way of an apology. "I should have been watching where I was going."

Surprised by his strength, Gail tilted her head back and gazed up at him. Eyes the color of a clear morning sky gazed down on her. His irises were not just blue, they were dotted with flecks of gold. How had she never noticed this before?

Gathering her wits, she took a quick step back, catching a better look at him. Freshly shaven, Levi was dressed in jeans, boots and a plaid checkered work shirt with the sleeves rolled to the elbows.

Inhaling sharply to clear her head, she lifted a hand to straighten her *kapp*, which had shifted in the fall. "It was my fault for being in a hurry. I just needed a breath of air." She fanned herself with a hand. "The kitchen is so hot this morning."

Levi bent, retrieving his hat. Running his fingers through his hair, he set it atop his head. "Sorry, we're late. Seth wanted to play with his puppy." He jerked a thumb toward the play area. She saw Seth perched on the tire swing, swinging himself around. The puppy bounced around, nipping playfully at his heels. Small barks and squeals of delight filled the air with joyful sounds.

The tiff with her sisters forgotten, Gail offered a smile. "That's all right. Breakfast is almost ready, so you two should come in before it gets cold."

He beamed at her. "Sounds good." Turning, he called, "Seth, come and eat."

Seth slid out of the swing and scooped up the dog. "Come on, Sparky." Crossing the yard, he gave his father a hopeful look. "Can Sparky have something, too?"

Levi shook his head. "Leave the dog outside."

Seth's expression clouded. "But he needs…" He stopped on the edge of blubbering, his bottom lip quivering.

"I think I can come up with a few bones for him to chew," Gail said, eager to soothe the child before the tears set in.

Seth's tears dried up. "Sparky would like that," he said, hugging his dog.

Levi opened his mouth and then quickly shut it. The expression on his face said he knew he'd been overruled again. He shook his head. "If Gail says it's okay, then it's fine by me."

Seth's antics brought out a smile. He was an adorable child with a lively personality. "He sure loves that dog," she said, leading the way back toward the house.

"He does." Levi easily fell into step beside her. His sideways gaze fell on her, registering appreciation. "I don't believe I've ever seen you in green."

Gail blushed. "I didn't think you would notice," she scoffed, bushing a nonexistent wrinkle out of her apron.

"Well, it sure looks nice on you."

"I'm sure in an hour, it will be stained and wrinkled," she said, referencing her penchant to turn every article of clothing she owned to tatters. Somehow, she always managed to attract every spill, smudge and tear the day's work in the kitchen and garden doled out.

Levi reached out, giving one of the ties to her *kapp* a little tug. "You'd look fine dressed in a potato sack."

The screen door opened, interrupting their conversation.

Rebecca stuck her head out, "Breakfast is ready," she called, waving a hand. "Come and eat."

Seth bounced in first, pup and all. "This is Sparky," he announced proudly. "He's mine."

Levi followed, admonishing his son to keep the dog out from underfoot.

Sighing over the magical moment, Gail dragged her feet. Levi Wyse had always made her heart beat a little faster. She supposed he always would.

Rebecca caught her arm as she passed. "You okay?"

Gail nodded. "*Ja*, fine." Drawing in a breath, she added, "I'm sorry I stormed out like that. It was wrong of me."

"It's all right." Relief lightened Rebecca's anxious features. "We shouldn't have teased you like that."

"It's okay." Gail added a smile. "Already forgotten."

After breakfast was done, the dishes were whisked away and piled in the sink. A last round of coffee was poured as everyone enjoyed the last few peaceful moments before hurrying off to the long day ahead.

Levi was the first to stand. "Guess I'd better head out. Those cows won't tend themselves." He motioned for his son. "Come on, Seth. We're going to work."

Seth grinned. "Yes, Daddy."

Gail readjusted her apron. "I'm coming, too." Whether he liked it or not, today was the day she was going to start learning how to do work on the ranch. Levi couldn't do the work of four men. The least she could do was help pick up the slack.

He gave her a look. "You're dressed much too nice to be going out in the pastures."

She glanced down. The frock she'd chosen to impress him with was entirely inappropriate for cleaning the barn, tending the horses and working with cattle.

I am such a fool.

"I'll change in a minute," she assured him.

Parked outside the barn, Ezra was tinkering with one of his old trucks. "Morning," he greeted, giving the newcomers the once-over.

Realizing the two had never been formally introduced, Gail remedied the matter. "Forgive my rudeness, Mr. Weaver. This is Levi Wyse."

Levi put out his hand. "Nice to meet you."

Accepting the gesture, Ezra Weaver barely concealed his look of suspicion. "Nice to meet you."

"Levi is going to help us with the cattle until I can hire some help. Please make him feel welcome," Gail said.

"I don't know if I'd agree with that," Ezra grunted. "What's this here fella know about runnin' cattle?"

Levi didn't blink. "I started working on this ranch when I was just a boy. Samuel Schroder put me on a horse and sent me out on that range from sunup to sundown. Everything I know, I learned from him."

"Is that so?"

"That's so."

Hostility settled between the two men, tense and awkward.

Gail stepped in, separating the two. "I won't stand for any arguing," she warned. "Mr. Weaver, I know you've been here a long time and I appreciate your concern. Of course, you do not know Levi. You were hired after he left. But Levi is a part of this family, and I won't have you treating him with any disrespect."

Ezra hesitated, then nodded, a sour expression on his face.

Unable to keep out of the conversation, Seth jumped protectively in front of his father. "My daddy's the best cowboy ever!"

Surprised by the child's outburst, Ezra Weaver raised his brows. His stern look began to fade. "You ready to fight it out, ain't ya?"

"Yes, sir!" Seth put up his fists. "I can beat you any day!"

Levi caught his son by the arm. "What did I tell you about fighting, Seth? That's never the answer."

Seth burst into tears. "He's being mean to you!"

Ezra Weaver crumbled. "Aw, now, don't cry like that. I didn't mean no harm. Us men, well, we gotta kick a little dirt to show who's boss."

Face swollen, tears dripping, Seth sucked in a breath. "My daddy can kick more dirt than you."

Levi took his son by the shoulders. "That's not an acceptable way to talk to an adult." He guided Seth around. "Tell Mr. Weaver you're sorry."

Gulping down a mouthful of air, Seth sniffled. Tears shimmered in his eyes. "I'm sorry," he warbled. "I didn't mean to do nothing wrong."

"You're okay, kid," Ezra groused. A humorless laugh pressed past his lips. "Got some spunk, that's for sure."

Having had enough, Gail folded her arms. "Don't you have chores to take care of, Mr. Weaver?" To make sure he got the message, she raised her brows.

"Yeah, I do, ma'am." Tipping his hat, Ezra Weaver ambled off.

Watching him go, Levi shook his head. "I apologize for Seth's behavior."

"Mr. Weaver is the one who conducted himself badly, and I intend to have a little talk with him later on. There was no reason to treat you that way."

"Don't be too hard on the man. He is right to be wary. He might be a little gruff about it, but he is just trying to make sure everything is okay. If our roles were reversed, I'd probably do the same thing."

Gail sighed. "I suppose I should be grateful for his loyalty."

"Loyalty goes a long way in this world nowadays." Giving her a smile, Levi turned his attention toward the work ahead. "If you can find a good man, keep him," he said over his shoulder.

Gail watched him go. Levi didn't know it, but she'd found her man, years ago.

He just didn't know he was that man.

Chapter Eight

"How long has it been since you've worked with cattle?"

Patting the neck of the cow pony he intended to ride for the day, Levi laughed. "It's been a while, but you never forget how to deal with those ornery beasts. It will be fine. I promise."

"You're not doing the work alone," Gail said, and doubled down. "I'm going to be out there, too."

Levi visually swept her slight figure. Truth be told, he needed the help. She had no hired hands, and it might take days or even weeks to hire replacements. Because the funds to cover payroll were mighty skimpy, all the job offered was room and board for the men and their horses; not exactly an enticement for such strenuous labor. The sooner they got the cattle sold, the sooner things would be back on track.

"I don't like the idea, but we have no choice."

"Mrs. Weaver is going to take over the cooking, and Florene has agreed to help out with household chores. Rebecca will also lend a hand. And Amity plans to keep the ledgers for the ranch, too. We're all going to learn what needs to be done and do it."

Pushing back his hat, Levi gave his hairline a good scratch. If nothing else, he admired her fortitude. Challenged, she'd refused to be defeated. "Sounds good."

"And I didn't forget Seth," Gail continued, refusing to waver. "Mrs. Weaver will keep an eye on him in the mornings, so you won't have to wake him early. At lunchtime, I will pick him up and bring him out to visit with you. Rebecca will watch him after she gets home." She offered an anxious smile. "I think we have everything covered."

He nodded. "Well, I guess there's no arguing with you. You're the boss."

"Mr. Weaver's getting the buckboard ready so I can follow you." Squaring her shoulders, she pulled herself up to her full height. "Today, I become a real cowgirl. All you know, I want you to teach me."

"Riding fences and looking for predators can be mighty boring. Not to mention looking for downed or weak cattle. That really isn't a woman's work."

Gail stuck out her chin. "Just because I'm a woman doesn't mean I am not capable of doing a man's job. Every day you're out there, I'll be there, too."

Levi glanced past her, looking outside the barn. "Then we'd best get going. Time's getting away and the cattle haven't been looked after in nearly a week. Best get out on the property and see what we find."

"You lead, I'll follow."

Levi tipped his hat. "Yes, ma'am." Slipping a booted foot into the stirrup, he mounted the horse.

"I think old Bob remembers you."

"Hope so." Levi checked his gear. A length of rope

was attached to the saddle's horn. A set of saddlebags carried the supplies he needed for a long day on the range, including a knife, a canteen of water, beef jerky, a rain slicker and a few bandannas used as face coverings when the dirt got up. A rifle scabbard hung on the off side of the horse, with the butt at horn height and the rifle's barrel angled toward the back.

"I'll meet you at the gate."

Gail watched Levi go, commanding the horse with a practiced hand. Hat tilted to shield his eyes from the sun, back straight, he handled the reins with experienced hands. His eyes sparkled, and a grin turned up one corner of his mouth.

Needing to get a move on, she adjusted her sunbonnet. Her normal everyday *kapp* was not suitable for work under a grueling sun, so she'd switched to a hat with an overhanging brim. A bit too tatty for church, it was too good to discard. Having taken the time to change her clothes, her old cotton dress with three-quarter-length sleeves would be light enough to keep her cool through the day. She completed her working ensemble with a pair of knee-high boots, hardly attractive, but practical.

Gail walked around to the side of the barn. Under a bright morning sun, Ezra worked diligently, loading the last of the supplies onto the buckboard. The wagon was outfitted with many of the same things Levi had.

Leading the horse and wagon forward, Ezra stated, "Not sure I'm agreeing with your idea. Your daddy would roll over in his grave if he knew you were plannin' to work cattle."

Gail climbed into the buckboard, settling on the hard

seat. The wagon was made for hauling, not for comfort. "Not to be disrespectful, Mr. Weaver, but *Daed* isn't here and we're shorthanded. I'm trying to hire a few men, but no one's inquired about the ad I placed in the paper. If we are going to make this work, we all have to make sacrifices."

"I could—"

Gail shook her head. A few years ago, Ezra Weaver had a heart attack, which meant he could no longer do strenuous work. The jobs he did around the ranch were things he could do at his own pace, without stress.

"Ruth would skin us both alive if you tried to get on a horse," she laughed. "So don't even think about it."

"If you say so."

Gail took the reins. She'd been driving buckboards and buggies since she was knee-high to a grasshopper and would have no problem handling the horse or the wagon it pulled.

"Giddyap, Bessie!" Unlatching the brake that kept the wagon from rolling, she gave the mare a tap with the reins. A complacent horse, not easily ruffled, Bessie knew just the pace to keep the wagon moving.

The buckboard rolled.

As promised, Levi waited near the gate leading out into the pasture where the cattle grazed. Dismounting his horse, he pushed the heavy iron thing aside, allowing Gail into the fenced acreage.

Waiting for Levi to re-latch the gate, Gail gazed over gentle slopes stretching as far as the eye could see. Leaning her head back so the sun warmed her face, she pulled in a breath of fresh air. The scent of mesquite tickled her nostrils. In the distance, she glimpsed the cattle grazing. As Longhorns had the ability to survive on the vegetation of the open range, this type of cow was an ideal animal to manage.

A smile widened Gail's mouth. Hope and promise wove their way through her heart, reminding her that *Gott* gave every living soul a fresh start with each new day, erasing all the misery and mistakes of yesterday.

She waved. "I'm ready. Let's go!"

Chapter Nine

Gail's first few days out were busy ones. The spring calves were ready for branding, a task that needed to be done right away. Rounding up and catching hundreds of the animals roaming across several acres of grazing land was quite a chore.

Riding on horseback, Levi located and herded the animals into a fenced-in corral. Once contained, the calves that needed to be marked with the ranch's logo were separated from the group and penned.

And then the real work began.

Standing with her hands on her hips, Gail looked over the group to be branded. Come late fall, they would be ready to go to auction. Part of ranching was knowing that some of the animals they raised would be bound for slaughter.

"I didn't know we had so many younglings," she said.

"Over two hundred, by my count," Levi said. "I'm sure there are some stragglers, but I'll catch them as I find them. Right now, we need to get these babies branded."

Lips thinning, Gail nodded. The theft of cattle and other livestock was big business to rustlers, and unbranded cows were ripe for the picking. It would be simple enough for anyone with a truck and trailer to cut through the barbed wire fencing and load up some cows in the middle of the night. That was why it was so vital to keep men riding the fencing and checking the property lines. The state police rarely patrolled the rural settlements, if at all.

"I'll do the hard part, holding them down," Levi said. "Think you can handle the brand?"

"I guess I haven't got a choice."

"Not really. The sooner we get started, the faster it will go by."

"Just show me how."

Nodding, Levi walked her to the branding station, which was a contraption designed to keep the cow immobilized while the hot iron tattooed its skin. A brazier filled with hot coals stood nearby. A couple of branding irons had been set to heat in the heart of the fire. A small table with a few other items sat nearby, as did a pail of clean water.

"Now, here's what you do," he said, and went on to explain. "I'll catch the cows and clamp them down. Once I do that, you will take the brand and apply it to the flank. Do not press too deep or hard, or you will burn them and that could set up an infection. You do not want to cause hide or muscle damage. You need to do it straight on, so the brand comes off clean and readable."

While looking over the items, Gail forced herself to overcome her nerves. The idea of branding an animal's skin was slightly unsettling. But it was necessary. She just needed to get on with it. The sooner they got started, the sooner it would be over.

"I'm ready."

* * *

Hours later, they were finally done with the first batch of calves. They were both sweaty and grimy, and near to exhausted.

Taking a break, they had settled beneath a few shady trees to have a bite to eat and something cool to quench their thirst.

"You've done really well today. I've never seen any man do the work better," Levi said, taking a sip of the lemonade she'd packed in a thermos tucked into a cooler filled with ice.

Gail shook her head. "I'm not made of glass, you know. I can handle it."

Tipping back his hat, Levi gave his brow a wipe before lowering it back into place. The hot sun was blazing down on them; the temperatures felt near to a hundred or more. "I'd forgotten what a trial this was."

"I guess you were happy to leave it behind," she commented behind a grimace.

He shrugged. "Oh, I had a couple jobs on other ranches after I left here. But I spent most of my time chasing the rodeos. Decided not to go into the events that would require me to drag a horse and trailer after me. Barrel racing and calf roping just didn't excite me that much."

"Why broncs?"

His expression lit up, and a grin split his face. "I know you probably wouldn't understand, but it's an adrenaline rush. And even though it's just eight seconds, let me tell you, I've had a few rides that felt like they lasted a century although the horse sent me flying the minute it got out of the gate. There have been times when I hit the ground so hard I was sure I was headed toward the hospital."

Gail shook her head, unable to comprehend the attraction men had to dangerous sports. Why would any sane person risk life and limb just to sit on the back of a wild animal for a few seconds? She couldn't understand why anyone would put themselves in harm's way on the hopes of winning some money.

As if able to read the expression on her face, Levi let out a little laugh. "It's a crazy way to live, I know," he admitted. "If I were a smarter man, I might have picked an easier sport."

"I remember how excited you were when *Daed* took you to sell the wild bulls." Now and again, Samuel Schroder bred a bull that grew up wild and completely out of control. These types of beasts were highly sought after by breeders of rodeo animals, and when a bull or horse showed a particular trait, it was usually sold off. Allowed to go with his friends to some of the local events, Levi had fallen in love with the sport. By age fifteen, he was hooked.

Now that they had reconnected as adults, Gail didn't hold out the hope he might change his mind about the rodeo. Levi was no longer a part of the Amish community, and it was doubtful he'd ever want to come back. And even if he did have any interest in her, there was no way they would ever be allowed to have a relationship.

If she left the church, she'd be excommunicated. Banned. Baptism was a permanent vow to follow the church. Taking the vow and then breaking it meant the entire congregation would shun her. That would mean no one could speak with her, share a meal with her, or conduct any business. Although it might seem unfair, it was a widely accepted measure and considered necessary to preserve the Plain community.

Torn in half by her thoughts, Gail blinked back unbidden tears. Why did everything have to be so complicated?

Oblivious to her feelings, Levi drained the last of his lemonade. "That sure was good. But we'd best get back to work We've got plenty more to do before the day is done."

Chapter Ten

By the time Sunday morning arrived, Gail was glad *Gott* had added time to rest at the end of a week. There was a lot more to wrangling cattle than just sitting on a horse, watching a herd roam the range, munching grass.

Riding down deeply rutted dirt roads—and often no roads at all—was not fun. The buckboard bounced and jarred across the rolling hills. Even on the flatter land, there were washouts, holes, cactus and other things that could take out a wagon wheel, not to mention deep holes dug by jackrabbits that could snap a horse's leg without warning. The rugged country was also chockfull of brambles, thorns and rattlesnakes, and skunks, scorpions and wild deer. She didn't know which was worse: the uncomfortable wagon, the blazing sun, the dirt blasting her eyes or the insects.

By the end of her first day, she was utterly exhausted, barely able to keep her eyes open as she cleaned up before dropping into bed. The smell of cattle clung to her clothes.

Up early the next day, she'd found herself in the barn, mucking out stalls and getting the horses saddled and ready to work. Then she headed out to check the fence line, looking for breaches. If there was a break or a weak spot, it had to be repaired right there. To her credit, she was handy with the wire cutters and pliers. Then back to the corral for more branding.

By day three, she'd gained a new appreciation for the cowhands, holding the men who could do such work without complaint in high esteem.

By day four she'd come to hate the pesky bovines and never wanted to see another cow ever again.

Day five was a repeat of the previous ones, except busier. There was always something to do.

Snuggled into a warm bed, Gail rolled over onto her side, dragging the quilt over her head.

Cracking an eyelid, she glimpsed her bedside clock. Much to her surprise, the hands read ten after eight! Church was at 9:00 a.m., sharp. That gave her exactly twenty minutes to get up, get dressed and make it downstairs in time to leave for the ride into town.

"I can't believe I'm late," she murmured, rubbing away the cobwebs of sleep blurring her vision. She had never overslept a day in her life. Never!

Throwing off her covers, Gail hurried to quickly wash her face before grabbing her clothes: a plain black frock, black hose and flats. Hair a tangle, she twisted it up and pinned it into place. A white apron and *kapp* added the last touches. The sun had burned her exposed skin, giving a pink glow to her nose and cheeks.

Hurrying downstairs, she discovered her sisters had already finished breakfast.

"Why didn't anyone wake me?"

Her sisters looked up.

"I guess we just got busy," Amity said, shaking out

the quilt she'd painstakingly designed and sewn on for close to a year. The pattern was a bright burst of yellow sunflowers on a white background and trimmed all the way around with lace. "The church's charity auction is today."

"We've been getting ready for this afternoon," Rebecca chimed in, unfolding a set of cotton sheets and pillowcases, all bearing a matching design. Embroidered by hand, each tiny petal was perfectly crafted with silken embroidery thread.

But that was not all the girls had prepared. Florene added a beautifully framed needlepoint canvas. Sunflowers circled a familiar saying: *Gott segne dieses Haus.*

God Bless This House.

Gail groaned. She'd completely forgotten about the events taking place after church today. Besides an auction to benefit Emma Kresh, an Amish woman who'd recently lost her *ehmann*, there was also a potluck meal afterward. She'd intended to bake Shoofly and sugarcream pies for the meal. Both recipes had been in her family for generations and were popular among the Pennsylvania Dutch people. But since she barely had a moment to rest, let alone bake, the pies had fallen to the wayside. She had nothing to contribute.

Ashamed she'd failed to do her part for a needy member of the community, she pressed a hand to her forehead. "*Ach*, I can't believe I forgot it was today."

Minutes ticked away, and there was no time to sit down for breakfast and have a bite to eat. She opted for a cup of coffee. Though her stomach growled, she'd have to wait till later for a meal. She eagerly sipped the dark brew. Warmth filtered through her aching body.

Amazing what a cup of caffeine and sugar could do for a person.

"I think we can forgive you," Rebecca said. "You've been gone from dawn to dusk every day. When would you have time?"

Amity refolded the quilt, careful not to let the lace sweep the floor. "This is from the entire Schroder family anyway, not just me."

A knock at the back door interrupted conversation.

Glancing toward the screen, Gail saw Ezra and Ruth Weaver. Both carried trays loaded down with pies.

"Here we are," Mrs. Weaver called. "All done and wrapped to go."

Gail gaped in disbelief. She hurried to help with the trays. Neatly covered with clear plastic wrap, the pies looked perfect. She couldn't have done a better job if she'd baked them herself.

"Oh, thank you! You are a gem, Ruth. I would have felt awful showing up empty-handed."

"She's been up since the crack of daylight, baking," Mr. Weaver filled in.

Mrs. Weaver laughed. "I know you make them for all the potluck events." Her expression shadowed. "Terrible thing about Mrs. Kresh, losing her husband so young."

"I agree," Gail said. "It must be crushing for her."

"I used your recipes," the older woman continued. "And I made a couple extra so there would be dessert for the family later."

"Perfect."

"We need to leave if we're going to get to church in time," Amity prodded.

Cloaks and bonnets thrown on, arms loaded up, everyone headed outside.

Levi was outside the barn, getting the horse and buggy ready to go. Built to carry up to six people and their possessions, the buggy was one of the newer models, fitted with headlights, taillights, interior lights and turn signals, all powered by batteries.

Entranced by the buggy, Seth ran around, clapping his hands with delight. Sparky nipped at his heels, barking intermittently. Together, the two created a joyous ruckus.

Seeing the adults, Seth came to a halt. "*Gooder mogan*," he greeted, haltingly attempting to speak the *Deitsch* language as he'd heard the adults do.

Levi shook his head. "Almost right," he said. "But you pronounce it like this—*guten morgen*." He sounded out the foreign words slowly.

Seth tried a second time, a little more successfully. "It means 'good morning,'" he finished, beaming.

Gail smiled. "Much better."

Tousling his son's hair, Levi grinned. "I thought I'd teach him some of the language I spoke as a kid."

Rebecca looked pleased. "I think that's a fine idea. He's almost six, *ja*?"

"In December."

"Excellent. How is he with his reading and writing?"

Levi demurred. "He knows some letters and numbers, but he's behind on learning to read." He looked a little ashamed. "That's my fault for not working with him. I should have read to him instead of shoving a tablet with some games in his hands."

"It's never too late to get him started," Rebecca stated.

"I'm afraid the delay's going to keep him back in

school," Levi said. "I wasn't ready to let him go, but I guess it's getting to be time."

"Speaking of going," Amity said, shifting from foot to foot. "We need to get loaded and be on our way."

"Of course." Stepping away, Levi patted the side of the buggy, painted with glossy black enamel. "I think this is one of the fanciest contraptions I've ever seen."

Of all the buggies they owned, it was Gail's favorite.

Ezra Weaver opened the carry space cleverly built into the rear. Resting on built-in shelves, the pies would travel safely. Amity often used the buggy to carry her goods to town, hauling jars of honey, eggs and other fragile perishables. To keep things from breaking, Samuel Schroder had had the vehicle specially designed.

"Are you coming?" Rebecca asked Levi.

Gaze taking on a wistful look, he shook his head. "I haven't been to church in over ten years."

"You were born and raised in the community," Rebecca reminded. "And even though you have not been baptized, you were a member in good standing. I don't see how that changed."

"And Bishop Harrison welcomes anyone who will listen to his sermons," Amity finished.

Levi's brow crinkled at the unfamiliar name. "Then Bishop Meyer isn't there anymore?"

"He passed five years ago," Rebecca said.

"I remember Clark Harrison," Levi said. "Didn't he run the hardware store?"

"That's him. He's bishop now." Florene rolled her eyes. "That man can go on for days and days with his preaching."

Gail shot her younger sister a warning frown. "Florene, please…"

"Well, it's true," Florene shot back "Those benches are hard to sit on for three hours."

Silently, Gail agreed with her sister. Come the final hour, her legs bothered her dreadfully from sitting in one place so long.

Levi appeared to give the matter due consideration. "There's a lot to be done here. I would feel guilty running off when there's so much work. I'd like to get it done before I head over to Eastland this evening."

"What's in Eastland?" Amity asked.

"Rodeo." He grinned, adding, "I'd planned to participate, but I got tied up with things here. I'd still like to go. I've got friends who will be there."

Remembering the meeting at the café with Bill and Shane Reece, Gail's spirits dropped. She knew Levi had plans he wanted to pursue after the culled cattle were sold off. Then, he would tip his hat and go on down the road.

"Of course," she agreed, attempting to sound cheerful. "It will be a nice break for you and Seth."

"Would you like to go?" he asked out of the blue.

She blinked. "With you?"

"Well, yeah. With me," he invited. "Matter of fact, why don't you all come? Then you can see what my life has been like since I left."

"What a fine idea," Rebecca said. "Except, I've got plans after the auction, so I can't."

"I'm also tied up," Amity groaned. She looked at Gail. "But why don't you go and have an evening out?"

"*Ja!* You've been so cranky lately, we could use a break from you," Florene prodded.

Gail turned the idea over. True, she would enjoy the chance to relax and do something fun. It would also give her a glimpse of the sport that had lured Levi away from the ranch.

"I'll make you a deal," she said to him. "Come to church with us today, and this evening I will go with you and Seth to the rodeo."

Levi grinned. "You got a deal."

Guiding the buggy up the street, Levi saw the church parking lot was packed full. The neat white building claimed a single block, separated by a neat, paved stone walkway leading to the nearby community center.

He gaped. The layout had changed a lot since he'd last attended services. Save for a single vaulted window on the face of the building, there were no markings, not even a single cross, indicating the denomination of the church. Smaller windows mimicking the design of the original helped illuminate the building in natural sunlight. Lawns and hedges bracketing the building were immaculately kept. A stone-paved sidewalk circling the building led to a set of double doors. The new building was pleasant, bright and welcoming.

"What happened to the old church?"

Sitting beside him, Gail gave a tight smile. "It burned to the ground quite a few years ago."

"Probably a good thing, because that old building was unsafe," Amity added. "This one is up to city codes."

Levi digested that bit of information. He well recalled the stone-and-wood building that had stood earlier, which was believed to be as old as the town itself. Dank, cold and dangerous, it should have been demolished years ago, but was allowed to stand as a historical edifice. The new church building looked much more inviting to the weary soul.

Though most Amish settlements in Pennsylvania and other states hosted Sunday services in the homes of congregants on a rotating basis, the Texas-based Amish were one of the few that worshipped in a designated building. Given the distance many rural families had to travel, it made more sense to have one central gathering place. An extension of the church was the nearby community center, which often hosted events for all townsfolk.

Finding a place to hitch up, Levi climbed down, helping each passenger out in turn. Taking his young son's hand, he bent close. "You remember what I told you?"

Seth bobbed his head up and down. "I think so."

"Be respectful to your elders," Levi said, giving him a gentle reminder.

The boy's face took on a serious expression. "Yes, sir."

Levi walked holding on to Seth with one hand and carrying a pie in the other, as he trailed Gail and her sisters on their way toward the church. Enjoying the warm morning, families milled throughout the crowded parking lot, everyone murmuring with anticipation as they unpacked items they'd brought for the auction. While the women were loaded down with food and items of their needlecraft, the men carried heavier pieces of furniture crafted in their workshops.

From what Levi glimpsed, there were many fine samples of Amish handiwork. There was no doubt in his mind that every item would sell.

In the community center, smiling women in neat black dresses and white *kapps* greeted them, directing them as to where the items should go. Inside, men and teenage boys hustled to set up tables and chairs for the potluck meal. Other women worked on displaying the donated items.

"Is there anywhere I can help?" Levi asked, handing over the pie to a girl working behind a counter set up for food preparation.

Giving him a shy smile, she shook her head. "*Englischers* are our guests."

Feeling less comfortable, Levi tried not to let her comment affect him. Looking around, he saw most of the men were clad in black, a white shirt beneath their coats being the only speck of color they wore. Worn over a vest, the men's suit coats lacked pockets or lapels or a collar. Instead of buttons, hooks or snaps allowed the coats to be closed, and suspenders, rather than belts, helped keep the pants up. Broadfall trousers and black boots completed the look.

Feeling very much out of place, Levi felt the urge to slink off. With his work clothes and Western-style hat, he looked like a gate-crasher among the congregation. It only made sense everyone would wear their best for such a formal occasion. Open to all, the auction was a chance to show the community what the Amish were all about.

I do not belong here.

"Maybe Seth and I should leave," he whispered to Gail.

"Nein." To the girl, she said, "Levi grew up Amish right here in town."

The girl offered a nod of apology. "*Entschuldigen sie*," she said, switching to *Deitsch*. "I meant no offense."

"Keinegenommen," Levi said, tipping the brim of his hat. None taken.

Blushing to the roots of her ears, the teen turned her attention to the pies. "What have you bought for the lunch today?"

"Shoofly and sugar cream pies." Gail handed over the tray she carried.

"Wunderbar. They look delicious." The pies joined the growing selection of scrumptious desserts. Cakes, cobblers, Danish and so much more were stacking up, waiting to be served to a hungry public.

Leaving the desserts, Gail and Levi rejoined her sisters. Together, they walked toward the entrance of the church.

Bishop Harrison stood at the doorway, greeting every congregant.

Holding Seth's hand, Levi stepped up. *"Guder mariye,* Bishop."

The bishop's forehead scrunched up. "I don't believe I know you two young men," he said behind a wide smile. Impeccably neat in his Sunday best, he was a portly man in his early fifties. "Welcome."

To help his memory, Levi prompted, "It's Levi Wyse. I used to come into your store with Samuel Schroder for supplies when I was a *youngie.*"

Bishop Harrison's face brightened. "Why of course. I recognize you now," he returned, clapping his hand on Levi's shoulder familiarly. "I haven't seen in you in such an awfully long time. Have you come back to stay or are you just visiting?"

Standing nearby, Gail answered for him. "Levi is in town a few weeks, helping us with the cattle."

"How thoughtful of you to help the Schroder *schwes-*

der," Bishop Harrison said, then turned his attention to Seth. "And who is this *kinder*?"

"This is my *boi*, Seth."

"Well, I'm glad you've both come," the bishop said. "I hope you will enjoy today's services and that you plan to stay for the auction."

Out of habit, Levi tipped his hat. "Thank you, sir. We're happy to be here."

"The day care is this way," Gail said, leading Levi through the unfamiliar building. They walked down a short hallway and entered a bright, cheerful playroom already bustling with children. An older woman was overseeing the kids, while a group of tween girls helped with the needs of the babies and toddlers.

"*Guten morgen*, Mrs. Halper," Gail said, greeting the Sunday school teacher. "We have a new little one for you today. This is Seth."

Blinking myopically, Greta Halper clasped her hands. "Aren't you Elias Wyse's *boi*?"

Many years had passed since Levi had heard his father's name spoken. "*Ja*," he said, perking up. "You knew my *familie*?"

Greta Halper laughed. "I did. Your mother was my *dochter's* best friend. I had hoped Grace would make a match with my son. Alas, it wasn't meant to be, and she wed your father instead."

Levi quietly tucked away the information. He'd lost his parents at a young age, and his memories had faded with time. There were no photographs of his parents, and the passage of years had blurred their faces and muted their voices. Now and again, a clear image from his childhood came to mind, but those were few and far between. It was almost as if they had never existed.

Nostalgia prodded. "I would like to know more about my mother's youth," he said. "Perhaps you'll tell me a bit about her when you have time."

"Gladly." Greta Halper turned her attention to Seth. "What a s*chönes kind*."

Grinning, Seth shyly hung back.

Bending to the boy's height, Mrs. Halper pointed to a group of boys about Seth's age playing with wooden horses. "Would you like to join us?"

Seth glanced up. "Can I? Please?"

Giving the boy a little nudge, Levi nodded. "Go on. I'll be back to pick you up after services."

All energy, Seth zoomed off.

"I see you have an *ehefrau* of your own now," Mrs. Halper said.

Giving Gail a quick glance, Levi shook his head. "Seth's mother died a few years ago."

"I am so sorry." Mrs. Halper reached out, taking his hand in hers. "Please know we will take *gut* care of your *sohn*."

"Danke."

In the main chapel, Levi took a seat beside Gail and her sisters on the pews lining the chapel. Like the outside of the building, the inside was undecorated. Save for two rows of hard, straight benches and a pulpit, there was nothing else. Sunlight streamed through the windows, warming the room and providing natural sunlight. As parishioners seated themselves, deacons handed out prayer books. As Gail had predicted, he recognized many faces, some more familiar than others. Several people gave him a friendly smile. He had not been forgotten, and the welcome bolstered his confidence.

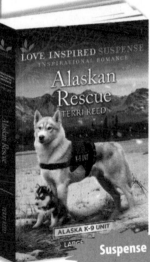

Get up to 4
FREE FABULOUS BOOKS
You Love!

To thank you for being a loyal reader we'd like to send you up to 4 FREE BOOKS, absolutely free.

Just write "YES" on the Loyal Reader Voucher and we'll send you up to 4 Free Books and Free Mystery Gifts, altogether worth over $20, as a way of saying thank you for being a loyal reader.

Try **Love Inspired® Romance Larger-Print** books and fall in love with inspirational romances that take you on an uplifting journey of faith, forgiveness and hope.

Try **Love Inspired® Suspense Larger-Print** books where courage and optimism unite in stories of faith and love in the face of danger.

Or **TRY BOTH!**

We are so glad you love the books as much as we do and can't wait to send you great new books.

So don't miss out, return your Loyal Reader Voucher Today!

Pam Powers

LOYAL READER
FREE BOOKS VOUCHER

HARLEQUIN® Reader Service —Here's how it works:

▲ If offer card is missing write to: Harlequin Reader Service, P.O. Box 1341, Buffalo, NY 14240-8531 or visit www.ReaderService.com

BUSINESS REPLY MAIL
FIRST-CLASS MAIL   PERMIT NO. 717   BUFFALO, NY

POSTAGE WILL BE PAID BY ADDRESSEE

HARLEQUIN READER SERVICE
PO BOX 1341
BUFFALO NY 14240-8571

NO POSTAGE
NECESSARY
IF MAILED
IN THE
UNITED STATES

As was tradition, services were held in Pennsylvania *Deitsch*, a dialect of German spoken mainly in the Amish community. Though rusty in the language, Levi gleaned the day's lesson centered around grace and forgiveness. Now and again, he whispered to Gail to request a clarification.

By noon, services concluded with a closing song of hope, sung by all. No music accompanied the clear, ringing voices of the parishioners, but it wasn't needed. Everyone sang together in perfect harmony. Again, the words were sung in *Deitsch*, but that didn't bother Levi one bit. He remembered the hymns from his youth, and sang with all his heart, basking in the simple pleasure of praising the Lord.

"What do you think?" Gail asked as they stood, ready to file out.

"I'd forgotten how peaceful it was to just sit and think on the Lord's word," Levi said, glad he'd agreed to attend.

"I'm ready for a break," Florene said, clearly looking forward to visiting with her friends.

"Don't go too far," Rebecca warned.

As the church emptied out, Levi felt a hand on his shoulder.

Surprised, he turned around. Bishop Harrison grinned. "I hope you enjoyed the sermon."

Levi returned a smile. "I did. Your message almost felt like you meant it for me."

Bishop Harrison beamed. "*Gut, gut.* I know some people grumble I go on a bit too long, but I feel the words need to be said." He paused, then added, "I do hope we will see you again."

Not sure he should make the commitment, Levi hesitated. Getting the cattle ready for auction was his number one priority. Even though the bank had given Gail a full month to settle the late payments, the days were slipping away. He still had to hire a truck and trailer to transport the animals, as well as take care of getting them sold.

"It's certainly a possibility," he said. "The Lord knows I could use some more time in the pews."

"As we all could," Bishop Harrison continued. "I also host a men's study group on Wednesday evenings. It's nothing formal. Just some prayer and instruction for those who are preparing for their baptism. You are welcome to come."

"Thank you, Bishop. I appreciate the invitation."

And he did. The sermon had filled him with an inner peace he hadn't experienced in a long time. The singing had also lifted his spirits. He'd also felt the fellowship and acceptance of the other congregants. Most everyone had welcomed him back with kind words.

"No pressure." The bishop chuckled in his jovial manner. "Sit in a time or two and see how you feel."

Hat in hand, Levi nodded. "Maybe I will."

"Gut." Bishop Harrison gave him a wink. "Who knows? The Lord might yet put the Amish back in you."

Levi reached out to shake the man's hand. "That might not be a bad idea."

It was true. Even though he'd only intended to stay long enough to help Gail get the ranch back in the black, he'd rediscovered living on the homestead had given him a longing for simpler times, when a man led a purposeful life dedicated to his god, his family and his community. It felt good to sit down at the table and bow his head over a hearty meal, well-earned after a hard day's work.

He had to wonder: if he decided to stay in Burr Oak, could he rejoin the Amish community?

The Bishop had put a bee in his bonnet, for sure. Maybe it was time to settle down and build a real home for Seth and him.

The notion gave him a fresh rush of energy. A plan began to take shape. When he had time, he wanted to look around and see what the housing and job markets had to offer. He knew the area, and the people. Surely, it wouldn't be hard for him to put down roots.

If nothing else, he'd also be closer to the Schroder ranch. Being within driving distance would give him a chance to drop by now and again.

Just to keep an eye on things.

Chapter Eleven

"What did you think of the auction?" Gail asked as they walked back to the buggy. Most every item had found a buyer and the sale had raised a good amount of money for the widow. Levi had bid on some handmade toys for Seth and a few other decorative items for his RV. The Amish widow and her family would be taken care of for quite a while.

Arms full of his purchases, Levi nodded. "You won't hear any complaints from me," he said, putting his items away. "The meal and sing-along was great, too. And getting to visit with folks I used to know was a real treat."

"*Gut*, I'm glad." Smiling, Gail added, "You didn't believe me when I told you I socialized."

Items tucked away, Levi turned, adjusting his hat to shade his eyes from the sun. "I was a jerk for picking at you," he admitted. "I really had a wonderful time."

"Honestly?" she asked. "You're not just saying that?"

Levi shook his head and made a gesture. "Nope. I mean every word."

"Me, too," Seth piped up, eager to share his news. "I made lots of friends."

"Thank you for inviting us," Levi added. "Best day we've had in a long time."

"I'm glad you both came."

"Me, too."

Now that the auction and potluck meal had ended and people began to drift away to enjoy the rest of their day, Rebecca had suggested a buggy ride so he could see how much Burr Oak had changed since he left.

Amity had gone to talk with a few other shopkeepers about the bishop's new decree on the use of computers and the internet in Amish-run businesses. Some shopkeepers were against the idea, while others were eager to embrace the technology that would help expand their reach to more customers. Florene had joined a group of friends. All the older teens stood in a group, eyes glued to their smartphones.

Watching them, Gail shook her head. Why didn't they just talk to each other?

Levi loaded Seth into the buggy, adjusting his car seat so that the child would be safe. "Now be still and mind your manners while we ride."

Seth nodded adamantly. "Yes, Daddy." He gave his father a pleading look. "Can we come back? I sure did have fun."

Levi smiled. "The bishop has said we can come again, so I think so."

"Yay!" Seth clapped his hands. "I can't wait."

"Sounds like he enjoyed playing with the other *kinder*," Gail commented as Levi unhitched the horse.

"I know he did. He needs to be around kids his own age." Guiding the buggy away from others parked nearby, Levi offered a hand to help Gail climb in. "Step carefully."

As his fingers curled around hers, Gail felt her pulse speed up.

Caught off guard by the unexpected reaction, she grabbed a handful of her skirt to keep it from catching on anything as she climbed into the passenger side. Seated, she smoothed out the wrinkles, making sure the hem fell to its proper place.

"Thank you," she murmured, waving a hand to lessen the flush heating her cheeks.

"You're welcome."

Levi climbed up beside her. To meet common safety standards, an orange triangle and taillights were affixed to the rear. The buggy was also outfitted with a simple braking system that would stop it from rolling into the horse when the animal came to a stop.

"I've been looking forward taking a ride around," he admitted.

Gail primly laced her fingers, settling her hands in her lap. "Burr Oak has really grown in the last ten years. More *Englischers* are coming in, and even some Amish from the northern states. New faces are always welcome."

"Never thought I'd miss small town living," he said, giving the reins a tug. The buggy rolled into motion, swaying gently. "I'd forgotten what it was like to ride in one of these things. Not so bad. Kind of relaxing."

Her nose wrinkled. "Better than cars, I think."

"I agree. Though I can't say I'm ready to give up my F150 pickup just yet."

Guiding the buggy through the afternoon traffic, Levi kept a firm hand on the reins. Though the horse was accustomed to the sounds made by vehicles, some drivers were careless when it came to the slower-moving buggies on the roads.

As they traveled, Levi's head swiveled every which way, taking in the sights. The wind kicked up, ruffling his hair. "I hardly recognize some places anymore. Main Street has really changed. A lot more shops than I remember."

Sweeping a few stray locks away from her face, Gail said, "It's why Amity wanted to rent a storefront in town. Her business is really taking off. She has even been able to hire someone to help her set up a computer to take online orders now that the town has an internet provider."

"I'll have to stop by and see her shop sometime," Levi commented.

The buggy rolled on. Because of the horse-drawn buggies and other wagons, gasoline-powered vehicles were forced to move at a slower pace. This didn't deter visitors, however. Amish goods had always been popular, and the town boasted a thriving tourist trade. Vacationers flocked to Burr Oak to purchase fresh produce and other handmade goods.

"Authentically Amish" was the official slogan of Burr Oak. It was even printed on the signs posted at the city limits. Amish and Texas were close to being an oxymoron, something that left some folks scratching their heads.

Gail watched as a car full of young women sped by. Top down, music blasting, they laughed and chattered. A few snapped pictures of the buggy and of her and Levi with their smartphones.

She momentarily dropped her gaze. It bothered her

the way tourists sometimes treated the Amish as if they were a curiosity.

Watching them go, she felt a brief pang of longing. Not having had a chance to experience *rumspringa*, she had no idea what it would be like to wear fashionable clothes or paint her fingernails with bright polish, as many other girls did when they came of age. As it was, Amish women were not allowed to wear cosmetics. Jewelry, too, was *verboten*.

Rumspringa was the time when Amish youths ventured into the *Englisch* world, eager to take a bite out of the forbidden apple. Though each community had its own rules, it was generally accepted that a youth could spend two years living their lives as they saw fit. After that time, they were expected to decide whether they would stay or leave.

Even though most Amish waited until marriage to be baptized, she had chosen to make her vow to the church formal when she'd turned eighteen. Her commitment to *Gott* was unbreakable. She'd never leave her faith. And unless she could find an Amish *ehmann*, she'd never wed.

Sometimes Gail wished she'd waited. Her sisters had yet to be baptized and could still marry outside the faith if they wished.

Albert Dekker had asked for her hand in marriage, as had a few other men in the community. As much as she'd liked them, she had had a difficult time even thinking about loving them. And though the bishop had approached her with the idea of a "family formation" match, she rejected the idea. Marrying an older widower who needed a wife to take care of his *kinder* and home didn't appeal to her.

She sighed. *The heart wants what the heart wants.*
And her heart had always wanted Levi.

A brief surge of emotion tightened her throat.

But all they could ever be was friends.

"Are you looking forward to the rodeo tonight?" Levi asked.

Shaking off her melancholy, Gail nodded. "*Ja*, very much."

Taking a breath and going out for an evening would be wonderful, and she looked forward to the experience. Though she had no interest in sports, she knew a lot of people did. Rodeos were usually attached to livestock shows and fairs, which were attended by most everyone. Some Amish boys were even known to join in. Levi could have easily remained in the local area and still chased his passion.

Perhaps he would have, had Daed allowed him more leeway.

Instead of encouraging Levi's ambitions, Samuel Schroder had forbidden him to participate. He expected the teenager to work the cattle, day in and day out.

"I'm sorry you aren't able to compete. I know you'd planned to."

Levi lifted his shoulders in a shrug. "It's okay. This one is not a large payout. Mostly I planned to ride just to keep my skills up. The big event I have my eye on isn't until July. That's the one I'm looking forward to. If I do win enough, it will take me and Seth through the rest of the year." He paused, and then added. "At least, I hope it will."

"Oh?"

"As a PRCA member, I've been invited to compete in the qualifiers for the richest one-day payout rodeo event of the year. It's called The Big Texan, and the purse is three million dollars, to be divided between competitors."

Eyes going wide, Gail gasped. "Cowboys are paid that much to ride a horse?"

Levi grinned. "Yes, ma'am. The higher the scores, the more that money goes into the pocket. There's even an extra bonus to be split between those who perform well."

"That's a lot of money."

"I've worked my whole career to be invited to compete in something this big. The event's going to take place in Fort Worth on Independence Day. If I qualify, I compete. Events like this only come along once or twice in a rodeo cowboy's life."

"And you're not getting much rest wrangling a lot of cows, I'm afraid," Gail said.

"No big deal," Levi said. "We'll get them sold in plenty of time to pay the bank. I'd like to see the look on Mr. Wilkins's face when you write him the check."

Her spirits sank. "And then you'll be on your way."

"Maybe." A shrug rolled off his broad shoulders. "Maybe not." He paused, clearing his throat. "I've had some things on my mind."

"Oh?"

Keeping one eye on the road, he gave her a sideways glance. "I guess I've begun to realize that I can't keep dragging my son around like he's so much baggage. Seth needs to go to school, make some friends and have that dog he wants. I can't give him that on the road."

"I know you've done the best you can, Levi. I can't imagine being a single parent and raising a *kind* on my own."

His expression seemed to tense as his jaw tightened. "You don't know the whole story, Gail, and I'm ashamed to tell you. What I will say is I've been selfish—wanting my own way without thinking about the needs of my child. Or even the feelings of others. I feel bad about the way I've treated the good people in my life. You're one of those people, and I'm sorry."

"Me?"

"Yes, you." He paused to clear his throat. "When you were a kid, I used to think you were a silly little girl—always following me around the ranch."

Gail blushed. "I didn't think you even noticed."

"Oh, I noticed. But you were young. And I was too busy strutting around like a peacock to pay you any attention."

"Let's be honest, Levi, I was a big pest."

"You were." He chuckled, then sobered. "But not anymore. You have grown into a fine woman. One I'm proud to know."

His words touched her deeply. "I'll always be your friend."

He nodded. "Anyway, I'm thinking about looking around Burr Oak for a piece of property. I think Seth would like to grow up in a small town. If we settled down here, he could go to school full-time. And he could go to church, too."

Gail's heart smacked her rib cage. Had she heard him correctly? "I believe Seth would like that."

"And there's another thing I plan to look into," he said, adding a hopeful smile. "The bishop has invited me to attend the men's Bible study."

Having overheard some of the conversation as they

filed out of church, Gail was pleased Levi had brought it up.

A tiny ember of hope flared. Was it possible he'd rejoin the church and get baptized? He hadn't said as much, but that was what she hoped was on his mind.

"How wonderful of Bishop Harrison to ask you, Levi," she said, careful not to reveal too much of her feelings. "I hope you will give it some consideration."

"I'm going to." His gaze brushed her face, a look as intimate as any physical touch. The tone of his voice said he was pleased. "I've got a lot of plans for me and Seth. I hope you'll be part of them, too."

Struggling to keep control over her emotions, Gail angled her head. Had she misheard him?

She dare not ask.

Tensing, her heart sped up as her thoughts whirled through her mind like a flock of birds set free into the wide blue sky. Though her joy would have had her shout out loud, she forced herself to stay calm. She had no doubts that the Lord was doing mighty and powerful things in Levi's life.

Feeling blessed to be a part of his journey, she said, "I will pray the Lord blesses you and your decisions."

"Thank you." His grin widened as he checked his watch. "Hope you're ready for a rodeo tonight."

But it wasn't the rodeo Gail had on her mind.

Was there a chance she and Levi might have a future together?

Reaching their destination, Levi parked his pickup within walking distance of the arena.

Keeping a firm grip on Seth's hand so he wouldn't lose him in the milling crowd, he paused to study the arena where the events were taking place. The scent of soil, manure and anxious animals all mingled together in the air. The evening promised to be pleasant as the sun tipped toward the horizon. In the summertime, the day lingered on until well past eight in the evening.

"Well, what do you think?"

Gail's smile wavered. "So noisy," she said. "I can barely hear myself think."

"It can get pretty crowded," he said, leading her through the swarm of people gathering around the food and drink vendors. Selling everything from hot dogs and hamburgers to cotton candy and other treats, the booths usually made a killing. There was nothing people liked more than eating as they watched the entertainment unfold.

And Levi loved every minute of it.

"Would you like something to eat?"

Gail started to shake her head, then caught herself. "Yes, I'll have something."

"What would you like?"

"I love those big hot pretzels," she confessed. "I had one at the county fair one time and it was wonderful."

"Then you shall have one."

Seth tugged at his shirt. "Can I have some cotton candy?"

Levi mulled his son's request. Even though he didn't approve of allowing a child that much sugar so late in the evening, he could hardly deny the kid his favorite treat.

"All right," he agreed, and led the way to the vendor.

"What color?" the man asked when it was their turn to order.

"Blue!" Seth called, delighted to watch as the man

operating the equipment expertly twirled the spun sugar onto a paper cone.

Levi inwardly winced as Seth devoured his treat. No doubt he'd regret it later when his kid was bouncing off the walls.

As he chose a soft drink for himself, Levi's gaze fell on the people buying harder beverages from other vendors. There was once a time when he was inclined to have an adult beverage. Matter of fact, he and Betheny had bonded over drinks at a party they'd both attended after a particularly intense competition that had seen him walk away with a couple of nice wins.

Leaving the food court behind, Levi couldn't help but think about Seth's mother. Her party-girl ways had frequently gotten her in trouble with the law and had, ultimately, been the cause of her tragic demise.

Frowning, he refused to think of the event that had sent his and Seth's life into a tailspin. He glanced at his son, so cheerful and full of life. Every day he thanked God Seth hadn't been harmed by her foolish decisions.

"Something wrong, Levi?"

Shaking his head, Levi smiled. "Not at all. Why do you ask?"

"You looked so sad for a moment."

"It's nothing," he said, packing away the memories he found unpleasant. The past was in the past, and there wasn't anything he could do to erase it. Building a future for Seth was going to be his focus from now on.

Treats in hand, they pressed through the crowd.

Levi led them into the stands. He liked to be up in the higher seats so he could see all the action in the arena below. The announcers were warming up the crowd, getting ready for the events to come. Competitors were prepping themselves and their animals. Wild horses and bulls snorted and bucked, fighting the handlers unloading them from trailers. Though not a large event, it promised to be an exciting one.

Pulling off a piece of her pretzel, Gail bit it daintily. "So, this is what you ran off to?"

"Yep."

Fresh memories filtered into his mind. When he'd first begun to chase his ambition, he'd started at the bottom, as all greenhorns usually did. He'd been thrown off his first bronc, but he knew he couldn't quit. Determination kept him moving forward.

It had taken him a few years, but eventually he'd started climbing the ladder as a professional. The money began to add up, and he even gained a little prestige as a bronc buster.

Though he had not stopped believing in *Gott*, Levi hadn't exactly thanked the Lord for his successes, either. Somehow bending a knee on Sunday became less and less important. And even though he made a living, he'd never quite hit the big time. He was, and probably always would be, just another cowboy hoping for a record-breaking ride.

Levi shook his head. He'd made a lot of mistakes. But his life wasn't finished, and many paths branched out ahead. He'd come to a fork in the road, and now had to decide which way to go.

Go back on the road, or stay in Burr Oak?

Glancing at Gail, he knew which way he leaned. The idea of marrying again had taken up space in his mind. *What if* he stayed in Burr Oak? *What if* he rejoined the church and got baptized? *What if* he asked Gail Schroder to be his wife?

Levi pulled back the reins on his thoughts.

One thing at a time, he warned himself.

He always tended to run ahead. If he were truly going to make the changes he envisioned, he needed to let *Gott* guide his actions.

Resettling in his seat, Levi attempted to focus on the events unspooling in the arena below. Rodeo action consisted of two types of competitions—roughstock events and timed events. Bareback riding, saddle bronc riding and bull riding belonged in the first category. Timed events consisted of steer wrestling, team roping, tie-down roping and barrel racing. Cowboys and cowgirls competed against the clock, as well as against each other. A contestant's goal was to post the best time in the event. If a competitor didn't place, they walked away empty-handed. Rodeo was one of the few sports that required an entrance fee but gave its contestants no compensation if they underperformed.

Levi had settled on bronc busting early on. The challenge of overcoming an angry wild horse sent a thrill through his veins. To earn a qualified score, the contestant rode one-handed, attempting to stay on the animal for eight seconds. If the rider touched the beast, themselves or any of their equipment with their free hand, they were disqualified.

As the bronc riding came up, he was anxious to see how other riders would fare. Down in the arena he caught sight of Shane and Bill Reece, along with a few other guys he regularly competed against.

Behind the gate, Shane mounted a solid black beast known as Midnight Express.

Wincing, Levi leaned toward Gail. "He's a bad one."

She shook her head. "I don't understand why a man would want to get on such a dangerous animal like that."

"You take a chance when you climb on any horse," he said, brushing off her concern.

"I know. But this just seems like asking for trouble."

Eager to see how his rival would fare, Levi let her comment pass unanswered. Like him, Shane Reece had been invited to the massive event taking place in July. Wiry and strong, Shane was an expert rider.

Mounted, Shane gave the signal he was ready. A bell rang and the gate opened. The audience cheered.

Set free, the bronc took off like wildfire consuming dry prairie grass. As he leaped and twisted with manic energy, it took him barely a second to dislodge his rider. Shane hit the ground, facedown into the dirt, and lay there, unmoving.

A collective gasp went through the audience.

"Ladies and gentlemen, please stay calm," the announcer ordered as medics and other men rushed in to distract the animal and attend to the wounded rider.

Stomach turning, Levi watched as medics carried Shane away on a stretcher. Even though he knew the risk involved every time a rider mounted a wild bronc, it was still shocking when an accident happened.

"Do you mind if we leave?" Gail asked. Clearly shaken, unease shadowed her expression. "I think I've had enough excitement for one day."

Levi agreed. "I think me and Seth have, too."

Taking Seth by the hand, he escorted Gail out of the bleachers.

"Will Mister Shane be okay, Daddy?"

Levi dragged a hand across his face. "We don't know, Seth. Let's hope so." It pained him that Seth had seen him tossed from a horse more than once. Every time, he'd managed to walk away on his own two feet.

They wove through the parking area and found the truck. Levi buckled Seth into his car seat and then slid behind the wheel.

Gail, too, climbed in and pulled her seat belt into place. "Thank you for bringing me tonight, but if you don't mind, I think this will be my last rodeo."

Heart thudding, Levi turned on the ignition. The engine roared to life. By the look on her face, he knew exactly what was on her mind.

"Getting bucked off is part of the sport," he said, attempting to explain away the danger.

"What if something happened to you?" Lips going flat, concern laced Gail's tone. "What would happen to Seth? He's just a *kind*."

Her tersely worded questions smacked Levi hard. "I'll be okay."

"Will you?"

"Of course."

Despite his flippancy, Levi's words sounded hollow to his own ears. Gail was right. He might have escaped with only cuts and bruises in the past, but what would happen if he were the one in an accident?

His gaze shifted toward his son, before settling on Gail. Seeing true fear on her face made shrugging off the danger of competition difficult. It was not just his own life that would be impacted if something bad happened.

Seth had no mother. If a bronc took him out, the boy would have no father. There were no grandparents to take him, either. Betheny had no family close enough to take an interest in her child. His own parents were also deceased. The few blood relatives he did have—distant cousins he'd never met—were back in Pennsylvania. If he were killed, who would take Seth?

The possibility his son might someday be an orphan all at once shook Levi to the core. He'd gone through the experience, and it had left him feeling rootless and at loose ends. The Schroders had treated him well, but he'd never quite felt like he belonged in the family. Perhaps that was because he was an older teenager, and not a small child. Had he been younger, he might have adapted better.

Still, it was nothing he ever wanted his own child to experience.

Gott willing, he hoped to be around to watch Seth grow up and have a family of his own. Perhaps someday he might even bounce his grandchildren on his knee.

Keep riding those wild horses and that might not happen.

Chapter Twelve

For Levi, the next few days passed in a blur. Between rounding up and selecting the cattle to be sold off and taking care of other chores, he'd barely had a moment to think. By the time Wednesday evening rolled around, he was looking forward to a pleasant evening. He'd decided that he'd be showing up for the men's Bible study group. Afterward, he hoped to have a moment to speak with Bishop Harrison alone.

Could he rejoin the Amish community? He'd never know unless he asked. If the answer was yes, the plan he had in mind could move forward.

The idea was exciting, and frightening. But it was also one he looked forward to pursuing.

So that he wouldn't stand out like a sore thumb, he dressed in a muted manner, pulling out a pair of dark slacks, a black shirt and a pair of boots that weren't Western-style. His colorful shirts and blue jeans just didn't mesh with the more conservatively dressed members. He wanted to show some respect toward the church and its congregants.

As he put on his clothes, Levi's thoughts shifted to

the news he'd received earlier in the week. The shadow of Shane's accident was still on his mind. His friend had suffered intense neck and back damage. The injuries had effectively ended Shane's career. With prayer and determination, he might walk again. But his days as a rodeo cowboy had ended abruptly.

Levi shook his head. *That could just as easily have been me.*

Not for the first time, he began to consider the fact that it might be time to retire. The idea of going back to a life he'd abandoned both frightened and excited him. Back when he was a teenager, he'd found the Amish lifestyle too restrictive and regimented. Now that he was an older man with some experience of the real world, he discovered that he liked the idea of leading a simple life: up before sunrise, putting in a hard day's work and giving the Lord thanks on Sunday.

Maybe there is a place for me and Seth here in Burr Oak.

A knock on the door captured his attention.

Buttoning his cuffs, Levi hurried to open the front door.

Gail stood outside. "I've come to get Seth." She lifted the book she held. "I've also brought you your Bible. I noticed you didn't have one last Sunday and I thought you might want the one *Mamm* gave you when you first came to live with us. It took a bit of digging, but I found it."

Surprised the family had held on to his belongings, Levi accepted her offering. When he'd packed to leave the ranch, he wasn't able to take everything he owned. Not much fit in his small suitcase and many items were left behind, including his Bible.

"Thank you for going through the trouble of finding it. And thank you for keeping it all these years. I won't leave it behind again."

She eyed his clothes, grinning. "You look nice. Almost Plain. Just need to grow your hair out and you'd look Amish again."

He ran a nervous hand through his hair, slicked back with a little gel. "Not too much?"

"Not at all."

Levi stepped back, glancing into the back bedroom. Seth lay on his bunk with his puppy, laboriously copying the letters Rebecca had written out for him on sheets of paper. Determined to read and write, he worked diligently.

"Seth, Gail's going to watch you while I go into town."

Putting aside his pencil, Seth slid off his bed. Agile despite the fact he was threatening to turn into all legs, Sparky followed close behind.

"Can we play checkers?" Seth asked, hopping down the narrow steps.

Gail smiled. "Of course. I've got some more games, too."

"I'm afraid Seth's fallen in love with those board games," Levi said.

"They're good for the mind." Gail tapped her forehead. "Keeps you sharp."

"A lot better for him than playing on his tablet," Levi said.

"We'll feed him some supper and keep him busy."

"Sounds good." Stepping out of the RV, Levi shut the door before bending to give his son a hug. "I'll be back as soon as I can."

"Have a nice evening," Gail said, waving him off.

Waving back, Levi headed to his truck. He climbed into his pickup and headed toward town. He pulled into the church parking lot. Aside from buggies and a row of neatly parked bicycles, there were not any other gas-powered vehicles.

Times really had changed. According to Gail, many of the Plain folks had updated to propane or gas-powered appliances, solar panels for lighting and other conveniences that wouldn't have been allowed under the former bishop. From what he'd seen, Bishop Harrison was in tune not only with modern times, but with ideas on how best to allow its conveniences to be used by the congregation.

A few other men were heading into the church, so Levi followed them inside. They gave him an odd look but said nothing. Passing the chapel and then the nursery where Seth had played the Sunday before, Levi stepped through a small antechamber leading to an informal conference room.

A group of men were seated in chairs set up in a circle. Everyone glanced up as he entered. The bishop stood in the center of the circle.

"*Ach*," one man said, whispering sotto voce. "Is that the *Englischer*?"

Bishop Harrison shut his Bible and stepped away from the gathering. "Levi, I'm glad you came," he said and directed him back into the antechamber. "I need to have a word with you for a moment." He closed the door behind him.

Puzzled, Levi glanced at the older man. "Was I not supposed to come?"

Bishop Harrison gave him a smile that didn't reach

his eyes. "I'm sorry to tell you this, but I have to rescind the invitation."

Levi blinked. "Why?"

He hesitated. "An extenuating circumstance seems to have arisen."

Levi's insides knotted. "I see. And that would be?"

The older man sighed. "It has come to my attention you aren't exactly a widower."

His brows rose. "Who told you that?"

"One of my ministers—I won't say who—has a relative living in Reno, Nevada—where I believe you also had a home a few years ago?"

Levi tightened his grip on his Bible. Telling a lie would be unacceptable on all levels. "Yes."

"According to what he tells me, you divorced your wife."

Levi's insides twisted. Now that the cat was out of the bag, there was no reason to lie about it. It was, after all, public record.

"I did," he said, and then added, "Betheny died a few days after the final decree."

Bishop Harrison's mouth puckered with disapproval. "Was there a reason you couldn't honor your vows to the woman you married and who bore you a *kind*?"

Well, here it was. The shame he'd so desperately tried to hide. No reason to lie or try to cover it up. The truth always came out.

"Yes, there was. Betheny was not a good mother."

"I see. Do you mind if I ask why?"

Levi refused to flinch. "She put our son's life in danger more than once." Drawing back his shoulders, he pressed on. "I did what I thought was right to save my child. I won't apologize for that, either, Bishop."

Silent a moment, Bishop Harrison nodded. "Thank you for being honest with me, Levi."

"If I had to do it all over again, I would. And if what I did was wrong, then I will stand up on my judgment day and answer to *Gott*. I know I made a lot of mistakes, but I'm trying to turn my life over to the Lord in the hopes *He* will make me a better man. If the church of my parents and their parents before them will not have me, I'll find one that will."

Save for a few extenuating circumstances, divorce was frowned down on by the Amish. Once two people were married, they were expected to stay together until death parted them. That had been his intention when he married Seth's mother. Unfortunately, the union was a disaster.

"I'm not trying to punish you," the bishop said in his own defense. "Given what you've just told me, I'd certainly be willing to reconsider the matter of your suitability to be baptized."

Levi pursed his lips. "Don't concern yourself, Bishop. Seth's mother paid for her mistakes with her life, and I would prefer she be allowed to rest in peace. As for myself, after I get the Schroder cattle to auction, I think me and my son will be leaving town."

Levi walked out the church building, and back to his truck. He slammed a hand on the side of the vehicle, frustrated with the situation he'd just encountered.

"Here I am trying to make changes to my life, and no one will let me," he muttered as he slid behind the wheel. Insides knotting, he stared ahead, seeing nothing except the mess he'd made of his life.

Doubt crept in, devouring hope. Caught between two worlds, fitting in neither, what was he to do now?

What if *Gott* had written him off as a lost cause?

"Stop it," he whispered, heaving a fortifying breath. "There are no easy fixes."

Focusing on his heartbeat, Levi cleared his mind of negative thoughts.

Yesterday was gone. All he could do was focus on a new day. Maybe things would go right. Or maybe they would go wrong. But true faith meant putting aside ego and submitting his stubborn will to a higher power. He needed to show he was ready to live a better life.

Clasping his hands, he bowed his head. "Dear Lord, I've strayed so far," he whispered, struggling to find the right words. "I ask Your forgiveness. Please, show me the way I need to go."

Chapter Thirteen

Twirling and throwing his rope, Levi took only minutes to capture a wandering heifer and guide her back to the safety of the herd. His horse, a fifteen-year-old gelding named Bob, was trained to work cattle since he was old enough to be broke to a saddle. Wily in the ways of stubborn bovines, Bob had a knack for moving and cutting cows, and waded through an entire herd without blinking an eye.

"Hey, cow, be still."

Sliding off his horse to set the heifer free, Levi barely noticed the twinge in his left leg. Lowing with offense, the animal trotted off, slapping flies off her rear with a bobbed tail.

He gathered his rope and watched her go. Not having worked with cattle in years, he was a little rusty, but his aim was getting better. He caught more than he missed, which was a switch from missing more than he caught.

He hooked the rope to the side of his saddle and lifted his hat, mopping his brow with a handkerchief. It was nearing noon, and the heat had climbed. June was one of the wettest months of the year, but it could also be hot. Come summer, the temperature would easily climb past a hundred.

Levi gazed out over the pastureland. Miles of buffalo grass and other flora mingled with stubby bushes. Towering trees dotted the wide-open plains. During the high summer, the rich-soil bottomlands along the creeks and rivers were verdant and teeming with an abundance of critters. Known for their hardiness, Texas Longhorns could forage on brush and survive for days without water.

He sighed. "Better get back to it, Bob."

Tucking away his handkerchief, Levi resettled his hat before grabbing the saddle horn and hitching a boot into the stirrup. Getting up and down on a horse all day was a tough workout. For the first week, he'd gritted his teeth through the aches.

Giving his horse a little tap with his spur, Levi let the horse have its own lead, trailing cattle at a leisurely pace. Cows were stubborn critters, and they usually got their way. Had the ranch been at full staff, there would have been more than one man working. A good cowboy could handle several hundred cows, but there was more to keeping up with cattle than just sitting on a horse. A man had to keep an eye out for predators, pregnant cows and foundling calves, among so many other duties. Normally there were three hands working the range, now whittled down to one.

Having settled on which cattle would be sold, Levi had started to corral those that would be going. Next week, he'd load the bovines on a truck and take them to be sold. The money generated by the sale would put the ranch back into the black. After that, he expected to hook up the travel trailer and head to Fort Worth to wait out the finals for The Big Texan rodeo. Once that event was over, he'd continue to follow the summer circuit before finding a place to park for the winter.

Staying in Burr Oak was no longer an option.

Life had a way of throwing a wrench in a man's plans. All he could do was find another path to walk. The one he'd picked had come to a dead end.

Story of my life.

The breeze kicked up. Stray clouds swept across the sun, ominously darkening the sky.

Reining the horse around, Levi headed toward a nearby gathering of sturdy oaks. The overhanging limbs provided a break from the heat and a chance to rest. Sliding off his horse, Levi let the lead fall. Old Bob would graze nearby.

"Datt! Datt!" The sound of a child's voice in the distance caught his ear.

Levi hove around, glimpsing Gail guiding her buckboard along a dirt-packed road. His heart skipped a beat as the pleasure he felt from the sight of her warmed his soul. She was beautiful and generous to a fault.

Seeing him, Gail rose, waving. "Levi!" she called. "Come and eat!"

Levi returned the wave. Gail worked in the mornings checking the fence line, and usually headed home around eleven to change out horses and pick up Seth for lunch. Given the heat and miles ridden in a single day, the horses needed rest, as did the people. Gail and Seth were always a welcome sight. Taking an hour's break gave him a chance to spend some time with them. It was the best part of his day, and he looked forward to the precious moments.

Gail pulled the wagon nearby, setting the brake before climbing down. Seth jumped down, rushing to give his father a big hug. Seth's puppy barked to be let down from the buckboard.

"Hi!" he greeted, throwing his small arms around Levi's neck.

Levi ruffled his son's hair. At such a young age, the boy had no trouble learning a new language, and was well on his way to becoming bilingual. He'd even asked if he could dress like the other Amish boys in church. Though it pained him, Levi had gently explained they were not Amish, but that he'd think about it. His reply had satisfied the child for the time being.

"Hallo, mein sohn." Levi hugged his child back and put him down. The frisky young dog barked and jumped, begging for attention.

"He wants to play."

He laughed. "Then go play."

The two youngsters, boy and canine, bounded between the trees, running off some energy.

"Be careful, Seth, and stay away from the high brush," Levi called.

"I hope you're hungry," Gail said, taking out an old blanket and spreading it on the ground in a nice shady spot. "Mrs. Weaver outdid herself today." She headed back to the wagon and lifted the enormous picnic basket riding in the back of the buckboard.

Levi hurried to help her. "Here, let me."

"Danke."

Gail smoothed out her skirt and sat down on the blanket. As she untied her sunbonnet, her sleeve accidentally snagged a long bobby pin holding her *kapp* in place. Her carefully tucked bun unraveled.

"*Ach*, my goodness!" Searching for her stray pins, she hurried to put her hair back in place.

Watching Gail struggle with her hair, Levi shifted in his place. Even when they were children, he'd rarely seen her with her hair down. The locks fell halfway down her back, covering her shoulders with a cascade of glorious curls. With her hair up, Gail was a pretty girl. Now, she was stunning. Though she wore a bonnet to protect her face from the sun, her cheeks glowed with a touch of color. Working as hard as any man, she'd put her heart and soul into keeping her family's legacy alive.

Gail noticed his stare. "Something wrong?" Winding her hair back into a bun, she pinned her *kapp* back into place.

Realizing he'd been rude, Levi quickly dropped his gaze. "Nothing."

"It's such a fright," she said, blowing out an exasperated breath. "How I wish I could cut it off and wear it short."

"You wouldn't want to do that."

"Hair is for an *ehmann*." A momentary shadow of sadness flickered across her face as she exhaled sharply. "As I don't have one, I shouldn't have to worry about keeping it long. I wish the *Ordnung* would allow single women to cut their hair. Just as single men don't wear beards."

"Short hair on you would be a shame," he said, carefully measuring his words.

Opening the basket, Gail spread out a napkin and unpacked the food. "Maybe," she said, speaking noncommittally. "The bishop is working on putting together a pen pal program with a Pennsylvania-based congregation to encourage more matches."

Jealousy kicked in. Levi remembered the announcement but hadn't paid it much attention. Since the Burr Oak community was small, the idea was to widen the net in the hope of adding to the Amish population by encouraging matches with other members of the Old Order throughout the country.

"Are you going to sign up?" he asked, without directly looking her in the eyes.

Lifting the foil off a plate of fried chicken, Gail shrugged. "I've given it some thought. Amity has, too, and she's encouraged me to do so." She laughed, but the sound held little mirth. "She says if I don't find a man soon, I'll be an *alt maedel*."

Levi remained silent. He knew that he had no right to make a claim for her affections.

The brief silence that ensued was broken by Seth, who was ready to eat. Plopping down on the blanket, he settled Sparky near his side. "Can Sparky have a bone?"

Gail shook her head. "Chicken bones aren't good for dogs," she informed the boy. "But I've got a pork rib here from last night's supper that ought to do fine."

Levi gaped at the feast she unpacked. Besides fried chicken, she'd brought homemade potato salad, deviled eggs and slices of chocolate cake covered in a layer of thick icing. There was also a thermos of cold, sweet tea to wash it all down.

"That's almost too much for one man," he said, accepting a heaped plate. "If I keep eating like this, I'll need new pants soon." Neither Gail nor Mrs. Weaver believed in cooking light, and they loaded their food with tons of real cream, butter, sugar and bacon grease.

Forking up a bite of potato salad, Gail chewed and swallowed before answering. "I'll just have to let those pants out so they'll fit."

Going after the drumstick on his plate, Levi bit into the crispy chicken. "I might have to take you up on that," he said, finishing it before helping himself to a glass of ice-cold tea.

Gail gazed into the distance, eyeing the grazing cattle. "You deserve to eat well. It takes a lot of effort, keeping this herd healthy. I must admit I never really knew how much work it involved in raising cattle. And you are one man doing the work of three or four."

Popping a deviled egg in his mouth, Levi swallowed and wiped his fingers on a napkin. "You work just as hard. Riding that fence line, looking for predators and downed cows and calves is not easy. Not only that, but you also run horses back and forth and take care of Seth. That can't be easy since I know he's a handful."

Catching his remark, Seth shook his head. "I'm being good, *Datt*. I help with the horses and the barn."

Her expression warming, Gail patted the child's shoulder. "It's true. He is good with the animals and doesn't mind a bit helping me muck out the stalls or curry the horses. Best little helper I've ever had."

Hearing her praise, Seth beamed with pride. "I'm a big kid now," he bragged. "Florene lets me feed the bunnies, too. Sometimes, they let me pet them. And the billy goat, it follows me around, too."

Levi laughed. "Just as long as you don't want to make a pet out of one, that's fine."

"We'll make a rancher out of him yet," Gail said, laughing.

Levi impulsively tousled his son's hair. He'd never seen Seth so happy or content.

Since the day they had arrived, Seth had easily settled down into their new routine. As the days passed,

Levi had watched his fussy, tired child blossom into a bright-eyed boy full of energy and good cheer. The change was an amazing and welcome one.

All four of the Schroder sisters kept Seth busy. To get the boy up to speed on his letters, Rebecca had even set up a makeshift school, complete with a kid-sized desk and chalkboard. After breakfast, Seth dutifully showed up for instruction, eager to learn his numbers and letters. The child soaked up every moment and couldn't wait to go to school with the "big kids."

A lump rose in the back of Levi's throat. Five years had flown by in the blink of an eye. Raising him had been both joyful and bittersweet. Joyful because he was so proud to be the father of such an amazing boy. And bittersweet because Seth hadn't had a proper mother to love and nurture him.

"Thank you so much for all you've done for him. And for me."

Gail offered a shy smile. "You're welcome," she murmured. "It's been such a delight having both of you here."

Levi had no reply. Falling into silence, he glanced toward the sky, peeking through the branches of the trees shading them from the heat of the day.

A sigh pressed through his lips. There was so much he wanted to say to her. She was everything he wished he'd gotten when he'd wed Seth's mother; a good Christian woman who loved the Lord and her family without question.

Much to his regret, he'd never be able to pursue a future with Gail. As an outcast from the church, she was forever out of his reach.

* * *

Finishing her lunch, Gail set her plate aside. Conversation had dwindled away, leaving each to their own thoughts.

The quiet moment was soon interrupted.

"Is it all right if I go play with Sparky some more?" Seth asked.

Checking his watch, Levi nodded. "You've got fifteen minutes, then we've got to get back to work."

Seth grinned and roused his pup. "Come on, Sparky."

"Don't go out of sight," Levi called after the pair. "I want to be able to see you."

"Okay!" Seth called back.

A wistful smile played around Levi's mouth as he watched the pair romp away.

Sensing he had something on his mind, Gail leaned forward. "You've gone so quiet. Is anything wrong?"

Forcing a smile, he cleared his expression. "Just thinking how fast Seth is growing up. I wish Betheny had—" Catching himself, he returned to silence.

At the mention of Seth's mother, Gail stiffened. Though Seth often spoke of his mother, Levi rarely mentioned her. From what she'd gleaned from his rare comments, Betheny Wyse's death was sudden and unexpected. Past that, Levi didn't feel compelled to share.

She frowned in frustration. Time and experience changed people. In the span of ten years, Levi had married, had a son, and then tragically lost his young wife.

Feeling unworldly and insignificant, Gail pressed a hand against her middle. She imagined that after taking an *Englisch* woman as a wife, Levi found her to be too simple, too Plain.

Levi noticed her move. "Are you feeling unwell?"

Hand dropping away, Gail shook her head. "I'm fine," she said, forcing a smile. "I was just thinking about all the things I had to do this afternoon."

Levi's expression darkened. His gaze locked with hers. "I wish I could do more so you wouldn't have to."

Heart thudding, Gail felt her pulse speed its pace. Mouth going dry as cotton, she licked papery lips. "It hasn't hurt me, and I've learned a lot. Maybe even more than I wanted to know."

Slowly he leaned back, taking in the surrounding landscape. "You know, I didn't think I'd miss it, but I love taking care of the cattle."

"I'm glad. Without your advice, I wouldn't have known what to do. You've been a lifesaver, and I'm grateful every day that you're here, and I look forward to many more."

Despite the hard work, she'd enjoyed the time they'd spent together. They made a good team. Given their conversation a few days ago, she hoped that would continue if he stayed in Burr Oak. She'd even considered offering him the manager's job, but felt it was premature to do so right away. She wanted to make sure the ranch was on solid financial ground first.

"About that—" Levi scrubbed a hand across his lightly stubbled face. "You remember Sunday afternoon when we were talking?"

She nodded. "Of course."

"Well, I hope I didn't lead you to think I'd be settling down anytime soon. I was just thinking out loud, you know. Chewing over my options."

Giving him a look of disbelief, she stiffened. "So, you've changed your mind?"

He shook his head. "What I had planned on for the future… Well, I don't think it will quite turn out the way I'd imagined. Think I'm going to stick with what works for me and Seth awhile longer."

Gail's insides twisted. The accident she'd witnessed at the rodeo was still very much on her mind. Thoughts of Levi being wounded by a bucking horse terrified her. Every time he climbed into the chute to mount one of the wild horses, he risked his life.

"I wish you wouldn't."

"It's my profession," he reminded. "I wish I had a better education, but I'm just an old cowboy. If I'm going to take care of Seth—and keep the bills paid—then I've got to compete."

Still a bit stunned, Gail silently digested his words. Apparently, what he'd said during the buggy ride meant nothing. He'd changed his mind, backing away from everything he'd said. Well, at least she hadn't made a fool of herself by offering him a permanent position at the ranch.

Lacing her fingers, she rested her hands in her lap. "I guess I'm not surprised. You've got a habit of walking away from the people who love you."

"That's not fair." Frustration knitted his brows. "You don't have any idea what I've had to deal with."

Heart sinking, she shrugged. "It's your life, Levi, and you have to do what is best for you and Seth. I am certainly not one to judge, nor would I." Lifting her gaze, she gave him a level stare. "Whatever plans you care to make don't concern me. At all."

Caught in the grip of disappointment, she turned her head away, gazing into the distance. The words he'd spoken had sounded so heartfelt, and so sincere. She'd believed every word.

I am such a silly fool, she thought.

Without warning, a child's frightened cry shattered the uncomfortable lull.

"*Datt! Datt!* Snake! I see a snake!" The sharp barks of a dog followed Seth's cries.

Gail jumped to her feet. Levi, too, sprang into action.

Both spotted Seth at the same time. Without meaning to, he and Sparky had wandered toward the wagon. A venomous snake lay curled near the right front wheel. Perceiving the child and dog to be a threat, the reptile raised its head, rattling its tail in warning.

Reacting like lightning, Gail snatched Seth off the ground, even as Levi hurried to retrieve the rifle holstered on his grazing horse. Sparky barked, jumping around, further agitating the dangerous reptile.

"Move, Sparky, move!" Cocking the rifle, Levi took aim.

Gail cradled Seth close. His small body trembled. Seth's dog remained steadfast, circling the snake until it twisted around. Instinctively finding an opening, the dog lunged and grabbed the snake behind the head, clamped it between sharp teeth and shook it violently before dropping it. Pleased with his kill, the canine nosed the dead thing.

Gail lowered Seth to the ground. "Thank *Gott* he's safe."

Reassured the danger was over, the boy ran over to examine the snake. "Good dog, Sparky."

Lowering the gun, Levi relaxed. "That was close."

Lifting Seth into the safety of the wagon, Gail pressed a hand against her chest to steady her pulse.

"Too close."

Just looking at the dead reptile sent a shiver up her spine. Despite the warmth of the sun, she'd gone cold.

Levi looked at her, as if there was something else he wanted to add before shaking his head.

"I'd better get back to work," he said, re-holstering his rifle. Changing his gear over to the fresh horse, he climbed into the saddle. "The cattle transport will be here day after tomorrow. I've arranged for the cows to be sold in Saturday's auction. Monday, you can take the check to the bank and settle your business with Mr. Wilkins. Once that's done, Seth and I will be on our way."

Nodding, Gail numbly returned to gather the picnic basket and blanket. "I'll be sure to pay you back the money you loaned us," she said.

"I'd appreciate that." Levi rode off on his horse.

Gail stood there watching as he got farther and farther away. Was it possible to have your heart broken twice by the same man?

Seems she was about to find out.

Chapter Fourteen

Returning to the house, Gail parked the wagon beside the barn. She put the brake on, hopped down and began to uncouple the horse from the harness.

Seth jumped down, as did his dog. He'd been strangely quiet during the ride back, and his little features were pinched. "Are you mad at *Datt*?"

Gail stopped cold. Seth had obviously noticed the tense exchange between her and his father. Observant and smart as a whip, he didn't miss much.

Wry irritation gave way to an exasperated sigh. "No, honey. I am not mad at anyone. I'm just sad you will be leaving soon."

Seth lowered his head. "I don't want to leave," he said, petting his dog. Tears welled in his eyes. "I want to stay here with you and Sparky." He threw his arms around her.

Dropping to her knees, Gail hugged his small body tight. She'd come to care deeply for the child. *I wish Gott had seen fit to make me his mamm.*

Blinking back tears, she lifted her head. As far as she was concerned, the spat with Levi was over. She'd apologize when she got a chance. She didn't want to lose him as a friend and hoped he would want to keep in touch after he and Seth went back on the road.

"I'll speak with your *datt* later," she promised. "Maybe I can talk him into letting you keep Sparky. Would you like that?"

Seth's troubled expression cleared. "Oh, yes. I sure would."

To distract him, she said, "Why don't you go inside and see if Rebecca or Amity have any cookies for you?"

He grinned. "Okay!"

Watching the boy go, Gail finished unhooking the horse, led the animal into the barn and brushed the mare down before putting her into a stall for the night.

With the cattle coming up for sale, she was anxious and out of sorts. The bank's threats weighed heavily on her mind. Being able to clear the back payments and return to some semblance of normal life would be a godsend. As for Levi, her emotions about him were conflicted and jumbled. Would it be better if he left? Or stayed? She was not quite sure.

Restless, she stepped out into the barnyard. A breeze winnowed through the trees shading the house. Unusually brisk, the wind had blown in scattered clouds that spat down a few fat raindrops.

Tipping back her head, Gail gave the sky a wary glance. Rain was coming. The trouble with Texas storms was that they could turn on a dime, going from nothing to seventy-mile-an-hour winds in the blink of an eye.

Keeping an eye on the storm's progress, Gail walked over to the swings. The limb creaked a little under her adult weight but held firm. Hands circling the ropes, she gave herself a gentle push. She'd played in this same place as a child, imagining her future. As the oldest, she'd always felt she'd be the first to snag a beau. She'd even planned her wedding, as all young girls did a time or two in their daydreams, picking colors for her dresses and building her future home.

Alas, it seemed her dreams of marital bliss would never come to anything.

The wind suddenly kicked up, howling through the trees with renewed energy.

Gail looked up. As much as she hoped it would clear out, the rain that had held off most of the morning finally made an appearance. Thickening clouds darkened the sky, obliterating the sun. The warmth of the day dissipated, the temperature suddenly dropping. A splattering of fat droplets struck the ground.

Protected by the overhanging limbs, she didn't move. The day had turned as dark as her thoughts. Across the barnyard, Levi came galloping up. Bringing his horse to a halt, he slid to the ground before walking the horse inside the barn. A few minutes later he emerged, heading past the animal pens toward the house.

Catching sight of her, he pulled off his hat and raked a hand through his hair before wiping perspiration off his forehead with the back of his sleeve. "Looks like that storm almost beat me back." He glanced at the clouds brewing above their heads. "By the looks of it, I'm thinking we might get a flood and some high winds."

"No telling what'll happen this time of year," she said, keeping her tone neutral. She wasn't really angry at him, just disappointed.

He replaced his hat. "That's what worries me. It's getting awfully black on the horizon, and with the heat clashing with this cool wind, I'm afraid that might mean tornadoes."

Gail shivered. When they came, tornadoes were one of the most devastating things that could tear across the landscape. Through the years, many homesteads had fallen victim to the terrible destruction of the twisters. The last storm had struck Burr Oak once, damaging several buildings along the main street before touching down outside the town limits and uprooting several large grain silos.

She grimaced. "I hate bad storms. They're so frightening and dangerous."

A shooting bolt of lightning followed by a clap of thunder warned things were about to get worse.

Gail jumped from the swing. "Better get out from under these trees."

Levi didn't have a chance to answer. The sky opened, releasing a torrent of water.

"Come on!"

Gail lost her footing, slipped and almost fell on the stone path. "Oh no!"

Levi made a grab, catching her before she hit the ground. "Careful, now." His arm circling her slender waist, he kept her on her feet.

Gail gasped as she regained her footing. "I'm okay."

By time they sprinted through the back door, the rain was pouring in sheets. Another crack of lightning, followed by a fresh blast of thunder, crashed in from all sides. The rain suddenly redoubled its frenzy. The wind kicked up, going from high to horrible. Clouds rolling overhead continued to conquer the sky.

Levi took off his hat and give it a little shake. Droplets of water flew everywhere. "So much for a nice day. Looks like the storm's here."

Close to soaked, Gail trembled. Strands of hair unraveled from beneath her *kapp*. "I haven't seen it come up this fast in a long time."

"It sounds horrible outside." Shaken, Amity hurried to get the battery-powered storm radio out of the cabinet. "Better find out what we're in for."

Florene was already on her feet, lighting all the lamps in the house. "Hope this passes fast," she commented. "I hate it when the rabbit pens get muddy."

Rebecca hovered over the stove, stoking in fresh wood. "Let me heat the kettle and get some coffee going. I think we're going to be in for a bad evening."

Cup in hand, Levi looked out the window. Though the wind had settled a little, rain continued to pour through the afternoon. Bolts of light illuminated the underbelly of the clouds, even as the electricity snaked toward the earth. Thunder boomed, rolling across the land like the feet of a mighty army advancing. The sheer power and force of the storm was a reminder of just how mighty and destructive nature could be.

After a light supper, Gail and her sisters sat in the living room, huddling around the fireplace. Tired from an active day of play, Seth was asleep on the sofa, covered by one of the many handmade afghans thrown across the furniture. Sparky had pressed himself against Florene's legs. Every time thunder boomed, the animal whimpered piteously.

Despite the incessant sound of rain thudding against the roof, the house felt cozy and safe. Kerosene lamps burning throughout lent the rooms a warm, comforting glow.

Gulping down the rest of his coffee, Levi cocked an ear toward the radio tuned to the local weather channel.

"The storm continues to advance," the announcer warned. "Several counties are under a tornado watch, including Tarrant and Brewer."

Listening to the rest of the forecast, Levi shook his head. "Looks like we're in for a long night. I should get out to the barn and get the horses fed and bedded down."

Gail looked up from her mending, needle paused midair. "But it's pouring out there. You'll get soaked."

Levi left his cup in the sink and reached for a rain slicker that hung near the back door. "The horses need to be fed," he said, slipping it on. "Besides, I'm not made of sugar. I won't melt."

Gail laid her needlework aside and stood up. "I'll go with you. I could use a break from sitting."

He shook his head. "No need for you to go out and get muddy, too."

But she insisted, slipping on a raincoat of her own and grabbing up a flashlight perched on a shelf nearby. "Nonsense. You will need someone to help you. Two of us working will get it done a lot faster than one."

Levi gave his chin a quick rub. "You're the boss."

Gail smiled up at him. "*Ja.* I am." She drew a fortifying breath. "Let's go."

Nodding, Levi opened the door. He was met with an immediate deluge of water. The rain smacked against his rubber coat. He smashed his hat down, lowered his head and dashed across the yard.

Gail followed fearlessly, keeping pace with every

step. By the time they reached the barn, they were both drenched.

Teeth chattering, she flicked on the switch near the door. Battery-powered lamps burst into brilliant light, courtesy of Ezra Weaver and his mechanical tinkering. She clicked off her flashlight. "At least we're not working in the dark."

Levi gave himself a shake, much like a wet dog would. He was cold, but hardly noticed it. His eyes were riveted on Gail. Her *kapp* drooped, and dripping strands of hair had escaped her tight bun to hang in wet threads around her face. Her skin was red from the cold. But with her sparking green eyes and upturned mouth, she was the most beautiful woman in the world to him.

His heart thudded against his ribs. Stepping closer, he brushed a few wisps of hair away from her forehead before tucking them behind one ear. "You're still pretty even when you've been out in the rain."

Gail blushed but didn't draw back. "*Danke*, Levi." A wayward smiled tugged up one corner of her generous mouth. "I'm sorry I was angry with you. No matter what you decide to do, I want you to know you and Seth are always welcome."

Levi swallowed hard. If only she knew...

"Gail, I—I—"

Unable to express in words how he felt, Levi gently touched her cheek with the palm of his hand. He moved closer, dipping his head. Gail leaned in, and he kissed her gently, sweetly.

He didn't know how long the kiss lasted, but abruptly, Gail pulled away from him. The meaning behind her actions was crystal clear.

"I'm sorry. I should not have done that. But I know how you feel about me," he said.

Visibly trembling, she searched his gaze with hers. "Maybe I loved you once, Levi, when I was younger. But I was just a girl then. As for now... Anything between us, it is not possible, and you know it. We are friends. Nothing more."

"I know you're right. Forgive me for saying things I shouldn't have."

Regret momentarily shadowed her features. "It's all right. I had to know, just once, what it would be like to be kissed by a man. But I will never break my vow to the church. Not even for you, Levi."

He nodded. It seemed no matter how far he ran or how hard he worked to clean up his past, he'd always be shackled to the *Englisch* world.

Just then, a perilous crack of lightning, followed by a blast of thunder, crashed in from all sides. Gail jumped. "We'd better take care of the horses and get back to the house."

She was always the voice of reason. "You're right. Let's go."

He hurried to close the double doors, locking them in place with a length of wood placed crosswise into iron brackets. A smaller door on the right wall led to an open side shed. Another door on the opposite side led to an enclosed room where the tack and other supplies were kept. Horse stalls were built toward the rear of the barn, as was the second-story hayloft. Half a dozen horses waited for their evening meal. The beasts were restless, whinnying and stomping with nervous energy. A few reared on their hind legs when the thunder blasted hard enough to shake the walls.

"Guess I need to get these animals fed."

Gail nodded. "Seth helped me clean the stalls this morning, so that part is done. They had a bit of time out in the corral this afternoon before we put them up."

Levi walked to the row of barrels where the feed was stored. He lifted the lid and scooped out a bucket of pellets. "Glad you got them in before the rain. That place is waterlogged right about now, no doubt."

"I guess you know Seth is all about the horses," Gail said, turning on the hose attached to a plastic tank.

He nodded and began to fill the feeders in each stall. The scent of hay, feed and horses mingled together, creating a damp, earthy scent. "The boy's been crazy about horses since he could walk."

Gail came behind him, freshening the water in the troughs. "What about his *mamm*? Did she like horses, too?"

Crossing to the next stall, Levi paused mid-step. Any mention of Seth's mother always caused his chest to tighten. Since his arrival, he'd done his best to avoid mentioning his ill-fated marriage.

He cleared his throat. "Betheny didn't go to rodeos for the horses so much as she liked the men who rode them."

An odd expression crossed Gail's face. "Oh…oh, I see…"

Levi finished his chore and returned the bucket to its peg by the barrel. *"Nein, du nicht."* Hands on his hips, he heaved out a frustrated breath. "There's a reason I don't talk much about Betheny. Seth's too little to remember much about her and, frankly, I was kind of hoping her memory would fade as he got older."

She cocked her head. "Why would you say something like that?"

Remembering his terror the night Betheny crashed her car caused Levi's pulse to speed up. "Seth doesn't know the truth about his mother," he said, feeling a rise of bitter acid scorch the back of his throat. "And I can never tell him."

A disturbed look flitted across Gail's face. "Something happened, didn't it?"

Jaw going tight, he shook his head. "I hate talking about it. I just can't."

Instead of turning away, Gail stepped forward and reached for his hands. "I feel so terrible for you. But keeping everything bottled up inside will never lead you toward the path to salvation. The Bible says whoever conceals his transgressions will not prosper, but he who confesses and forsakes them will get mercy. You will never be free of the past until you let it stop haunting you."

Levi started to reply, and then stopped. The silence was deafening. It took him a minute to realize the rain and thunder had suddenly ceased. The wind, too, had gone dead-still. An eerie quiet had settled over the barn and animals.

"Something's changed," he said. "The rain has stopped."

Gail's eyes widened. "Oh, please don't let it be…" Rushing to the side door, she pushed it open and ran outside into the darkness.

"Gail, no!"

Hot on her heels, Levi sprinted after her. It took him a minute to orient himself in the dark. Fortunately, the lightning hadn't ceased, and a series of flashes lit the landscape. Guided by the light, he saw Gail run past the barnyard, passing the trees lining the driveway until the gate stopped her trek. A clear view of the open landscape stretched out in the distance.

Catching up with her, Levi grabbed her arm. "What are you doing?"

Jerking free, Gail pointed. "Look there!"

Frantically searching the gloom, Levi focused on the danger looming on the far horizon. The wind suddenly spun up again, ripping his hat off his head. It disappeared, lost to the relentless wind.

The sound of something much like a freight train blasted through the night. Small, bright, blue-green flashes flared again and again as powerlines along the highway snapped. Illuminated by the lightning, a thick gray funnel had touched down. Barreling across the landscape, the tornado sucked up everything in its path.

And it was heading straight toward the ranch.

Chapter Fifteen

"That's coming fast!" Grabbing Gail's hand, Levi pulled her away from the gate. "We need to get into the storm shelter. Now!"

They sprinted in tandem toward the house. The wind turned vicious, scratching at their skin and clothes, threatening to push them off their feet. Fighting their way forward, they barreled through the back door with a crash.

"Twister on the ground!" Gail shouted to her startled sisters.

Everyone but Seth jumped to their feet. Blissfully asleep, the child had no idea danger loomed.

"The radio station went off the air a few minutes ago," Amity informed them. "We've got nothing but static."

"We've got to get into the cellar." Levi rushed to the sofa and scooped Seth up.

Amity grabbed a flashlight and the radio even as Rebecca hurried to douse the fires in the hearth and oven. Florene snatched Sparky, causing the dog to let out a surprised yelp.

The frightened group dashed out the back door and around the side of the house. Fighting the wind, Amity and Gail struggled to pull open the metal door that would take them underground to safety. The rain attacked with fresh vengeance, pelting the earth with a shattering attack of icy hail.

Once the door opened, Amity led the way down into the dark cavern, shining her flashlight down the narrow steps. Without hesitation, they all descended to safety. Pushed back in place by the intense wind, the door slammed shut, sealing everyone inside. As if angered by the defeat, the hail continued to drum against the metal barrier, filling the cellar with its steady beat.

Relaxing a bit, Levi looked around the enclosed space. Originally dug as a root cellar, the space had been widened into a basement for extra storage. Several custom-built shelves and cabinets overflowed with canned vegetables. A few foldable cots and chairs were stacked in a corner. There was even a first aid kit and a fire extinguisher.

"That was horrible," Rebecca said, rubbing a red mark imprinted on her temple. "I don't think I've seen it hail that hard in years."

Gail glanced at the ceiling. "Levi and I saw a funnel. No telling how far away it was, but it looked dangerous. I know we got the horses in, but I'm worried about the cattle."

"They're out in the open pasture, but they have a good chance of coming through just fine," Levi said, attempting to allay her worry. "A few might be injured, but hopefully they will stay to the low areas and not panic." His words sounded hollow in his ears. Livestock were often injured or displaced or even died during storms.

"May the Lord protect everyone in the path of these twisters, including the animals," Rebecca said. "I know Ezra was saying earlier he thought we'd have a storm today, but I didn't think it'd be this fierce. The bunkhouse doesn't have a storm cellar, so they'll be over soon, I'm sure."

"Still no news." Fiddling with the radio, Amity tried to tune into the local radio station. "If they've gone off the air, it must be bad."

Florene released the dog from her arms. Frightened by the thunder, Sparky cowered, slinking off to a corner to hide. "How long do you think it will last?"

Levi, who was still clutching Seth, cradled his son against his chest. "This could be gone in a few minutes or it could last all night. As long as it sounds horrible up there, I think we should all stay down here, at least a few hours. Just to be safe."

Tornadoes and Texas went practically hand in hand. The central and high plains of the state were part of the area known as "tornado alley," part of a swath across the country most likely to be struck. The thing about the twisters was that there was not one certain time in which they might strike, though midsummer was the most dangerous.

Amity exhaled loudly. "Since we're stuck down here, we might as well be comfortable." She pointed to the cots and chairs. "Florene, grab some of those, won't you? And Rebecca, I think there's a couple of blankets in those bags on that far shelf."

Everyone set to work without grumbling.

"*Ach*, these cots are so uncomfortable," Florene

grumbled, unfolding the narrow beds. She set down a few chairs nearby.

"Not the first time we've done this," Rebecca said, pulling out two heavier quilts that had gone into storage. She spread them over the foam mattresses.

Amity lit a few kerosene lamps, illuminating the chilled gloom with a cheery glow. The radio perched on a shelf spat nothing but static. "Music would be nice, but even the classical station is down."

Florene slipped her cell out of her pocket. "I've got no signal, either." She frowned at the display. "And my battery is almost dead."

Rebecca shot a look at the tiny glowing screen. "For once I wish that thing worked."

"The last text I had from Frida said the rain was flooding roads around town."

"If this keeps up and the old riverbeds start to run again, we could be trapped for a couple of days," Gail said.

"That's the trouble with the weather," Levi said, laying Seth on one of the cots. "Mother Nature's going to have her say. All we can do is hold on and pray hard."

Prodded out of sleep, Seth sat up, rubbing his eyes. "Daddy? Daddy?" Confusion turned his words into a high treble.

Levi sat down. "It's okay," he said, rubbing a hand across the nape of the boy's neck to soothe him. "We're down in the cellar waiting out the storm."

Seth's eyes widened with panic. "Where's Sparky?"

"Sparky's right here." Florene fetched the puppy and deposited him on the cot. All paws and ears, the shepherd mix was now at least thirty pounds.

Seth wrapped his arms around his dog, snuggling

into the warmth of his fur. "I'm so happy you're here," he whispered.

Moved by the sight, Levi felt tight fingers squeezing his chest. Seth loved that dog probably more than he'd ever loved anything in his entire life. Sparky was his constant companion and rarely left Seth's side. The animal was intelligent, instinctively taking a protective role toward the boy. Better yet, having a pet to look after had given Seth a sense of pride and responsibility.

"We couldn't forget him. He's family, too."

The storm door opened, bringing in a fresh rush of wind and rain.

Ezra and Ruth Weaver descended into the cellar, a clatter of heavy feet and anxiety hurrying them along. The storm outside continued its assault, pounding furiously against the metal door. Icy pellets sounded like gunfire.

"Thought we'd find you all down here," Ezra Weaver said, hacking a little into his handkerchief as he shook off the wet.

Red hair blown into strings, Ruth Weaver clutched a covered pan in both hands. "Didn't think I'd have time to finish my baking."

Levi stood. "How's it looking out there?"

Tucking away his handkerchief, Ezra Weaver fis[h] his pipe out of a pocket. "The twister didn't make far, and everything's holdin'," he said befor[e] the stem between his teeth. "But there's [n]o many of those things are gonna pop u[p]

At least the news was good. For mean the danger was over.

"We haven't had a terribl[e]

man said. "Last one I recall was over twenty years ago. Killed many people."

"Don't talk like that," Ruth Weaver said, frowning at her husband. "This storm is going to pass us by, the Lord be willing."

"*Ja*," Gail agreed quietly. "We should take a moment to pray."

As everyone bowed their heads, Levi sat and curled a protective arm around Seth and his pup. His son snuggled close.

Gail spoke in a clear voice. "Dear *Gott*, You are our shelter when storms come, and we are secure, no matter the danger. You are our defense and we will not be fearful when the wind rages, for You are ever near us. We humbly beg You to keep us safe. Amen."

"Amen," everyone finished together.

"And Sparky says amen, too," Seth added.

Everyone chuckled, which lightened the heavy mood. The atmosphere in the cellar was warmed and strengthened by the shared moment.

Sniffing, Florene glanced around. "Do I smell chocolate?"

dn't leave a fresh batch
ter," she said, holding
ave behind. "Is anyone

ether and grinned. "I
? She patted her thick-
count tonight."

e called. "I love those

oo hard for me."

t we have a propane

burner?" Rummaging, she located a little camping stove and matching metal pot.

"And if I recall rightly, we have plenty of tea bags and instant coffee, too," Rebecca added.

"We have some cups here," Gail said, pulling out an array of odd-sized mugs belonging to no particular set. She turned. "Levi, would you open one of the water bottles, please?"

He nodded. "Of course."

He lifted one of the heavy, five-gallon containers and carried it to the counter, to help Amity fill her pot. He liked the way the sisters bustled around, each keeping their hands busy and not focusing on the storm. Part of that, he felt, had to do with Seth. If the adults were afraid, Seth would be, too.

Amity lit the burner with a match and sat the pot on top of the little flame. "Tea will be ready soon."

Taking a seat at the foot of the concrete steps, Ezra Weaver made himself comfortable. "A soul could move in and live nice down here," he commented to no one in particular.

Ruth Weaver gave her husband a fond look. "You would be content burrowed in a hole."

Coughing, Ezra Weaver sucked on his unlit pipe. "Ah, yeah," he agreed. "I could fit it out real nice, add lights and even a little privy."

Mrs. Weaver sliced into the brownies and cut everyone a generous piece. "I made the old-fashioned kind, with plenty of walnuts."

Amity put bags into the mugs and added boiling water to let them steep. "Tea's ready for anyone who wants a cup. I hope you all don't mind Earl Grey."

Seth anxiously tugged Levi's shirt. "Can I have a brownie, Dad?"

"Just a small piece. And don't feed any to Sparky. Chocolate is poisonous to dogs."

"Okay." Seth hopped off the cot and went to claim his share.

Mrs. Weaver cut him a child-size portion. "Here you go."

Seth grinned up at her. "Thank you." Treasure in hand, he settled back on the cot. Sparky gazed at his young master through envious eyes.

Carrying two mismatched teacups, Gail offered one to Levi. "I think we all could use a little chocolate to help calm our nerves."

Giving her a smile, Levi accepted the plate. "Thank you."

They each claimed a chair, sitting side by side. Both ate in silence, listening to the chatter of her sisters and the Weavers trying to distract themselves from a stressful situation.

Though he tried not to stare, Levi's gaze gravitated toward Gail. Prodded by conscience and the need to make things right, he put his empty plate aside.

It's time. I have to tell her the truth about me and Betheny.

The storm carried on. The wind howled incessantly. Now and again, there would be an audible crack of lightning followed by an intense, thundering blast that shook everyone to the core.

Having perched herself near a kerosene lamp to read, Gail looked up from one of Rebecca's romance novels she'd dug out of a box. She enjoyed reading, and through the pages of books, she visited faraway lands, met fascinating characters and shared in their adventures.

Her father had passed along his love for reading. Once the day's work was done and the evening meal eaten, Samuel Schroder would read from the Bible, leading the family through their evening devotional. Afterward, as a treat, he read the girls a story, using different voices to bring the characters to life. Contrary to popular belief, the Amish didn't only read Bibles or other religious tracts. The library was a vital resource for members of the church.

Unable to concentrate on the plot, Gail lowered the book. Most everyone else had found a place to settle down, drifting off to sleep.

Except Levi. Having traded places with Ezra Weaver, he sat near the top of the stairs, wreathed in flickering shadows. Leaning forward, he'd clasped his hands, resting his elbows on his knees. Head bowed, he appeared to be deep in meditation.

Knowing he was unaware she watched, Gail took a moment to study him. He was clad in faded jeans and leather work boots, with the sleeves of his plaid shirt cuffed up at his elbows. Tanned and solid, he had the lean, muscular look of a mature man.

Completing his silent contemplation, Levi raised his head. His gaze caught hers.

Gail froze. Had he sensed her watching him? She wasn't sure.

Needing to stretch her legs, she stood. She laid the book aside and wove her way around the sleeping people, careful to disturb no one. Climbing the steps, she sat down beside him and cocked an ear toward the metal storm door.

"Sounds a little better out there," she said, leaning closer and whispering.

Levi scooted over to give her a little more room. "Sounds that way," he returned, glancing over their heads. "I hope the worst of it is over. The wind seems to be dropping."

"Let's hope so."

Levi shifted, his leg brushing hers. "Sorry."

Gail gave him a nudge back. "No need to apologize."

Pulling a breath, Levi blurted, "Actually, I do owe you an apology. I've been doing a lot of thinking, some of it out loud, and it led you to think Seth and I would be staying permanently."

She allowed a cautious nod. "Sounded that way to me."

"I meant what I said, Gail. I want to settle down and raise Seth, and I want to lead a better life. And I wanted to rejoin the church and get baptized, but that's not going to happen."

She shook her head. "I don't understand. I thought Bishop Harrison invited…"

Levi cut her off with a brief gesture. "I guess I'll just say it. The bishop told me at the meeting Wednesday night that I can't come back to church."

"Oh, Levi. Why didn't you tell me?"

"I was ashamed." Hesitating, he added, "I know you've never asked, but there are some things about Seth's mom I've never told you."

Gail nodded solemnly. "I suspected, but I never wanted to pry."

"I never wanted to tell you because I didn't want you to think less of me."

"Why would you think that? Whatever you've done,

I'm sure you had your reasons." She laid a hand on his arm. "You're a *gut* man, Levi. I don't see you setting out to hurt someone deliberately."

He visibly grimaced. "You might not think so highly of me when you know the truth."

Meeting his gaze, she tightened her grip on his arm. She could almost imagine the wheels in his mind turning as he selected each word. "You can tell me anything."

Levi's mouth tightened, revealing his inner stress. "Um, there's a certain sort of woman who likes dating rodeo cowboys. The relationships don't last more than a season or two."

Gail instantly connected the dots. "I understand what you're telling me. I am not that innocent, Levi. I know some young folks sow their wild oats during *rumspringa*. It's only natural."

"I'm not proud of my past," he said.

"If that's the worst sin you committed," she continued, trying to lighten his burden, "I doubt Bishop Harrison would hold it against you. I know many couples who had to rush the wedding and then say the *kind* came early. It doesn't make them bad people. Just human."

He raised a hand. "There's more. To an inexperienced country boy, Betheny was beautiful, sophisticated and exciting. And I must admit, I was proud that a woman like her wanted to be with me. But then she got pregnant with Seth."

"Ah."

He grimaced. "Betheny and I had no business getting married or having a kid."

Gail shook her head. "Levi, that precious little *boi* could never be a mistake."

"*Nein.* I can't call Seth a mistake. He's everything to me. The two of us together created this unique little individual. I just wish Betheny had been more…"

Sensing trouble in his tone, Gail urged him to continue. "What happened, Levi?"

He sighed. "Betheny hated being a mom. She missed the party life, traveling with the rodeo. Staying home and taking care of a baby was not what she saw as her future. So she drank a little, and then a lot more." He bit off his words, unwilling to go further.

Heart stalling, Gail felt a rush of anxiety. "Levi, go on."

His mouth turned into a deep frown. "Betheny had a bad habit of drinking and driving. One night, she decided she wanted to get out of the house and meet up with friends. She had Seth in the car with her. She didn't get far from home before she ran a red light, plowing straight into a semitruck."

Gail's hand flew to her mouth. "Oh!"

"Thankfully, Betheny had enough sense to put Seth in his car seat." He paused, and then added, "Seth was bruised but unharmed. Betheny also survived. But after that incident, I decided I had to take him and leave before something worse happened."

Gail sensed the weight of his guilt, sorrow and regret. It took a lot of courage and strength for him to share his tragic story. "I see."

Levi visibly flinched. "No, you don't. I'm not a widower, like you thought I was. I divorced Betheny because she wouldn't get help for her addiction, and I was afraid for Seth's life. The accident that killed her happened after we'd split. The bishop knows this and, technically, in the eyes of the church I am a divorced man. And that is not acceptable."

His words caused Gail's breath to stall. In that moment, the hard concrete she sat on and the chill in the cellar faded. "I'm so sorry."

"It is what it is. I messed up my life in so many ways. And now that I'm trying to fix it, I can't."

Gail trembled as her composure melted. A ribbon of warmth curled around her heart. "I believe you."

Leaning closer, Levi caressed her cheek with gentle fingers. "I had so many plans for Seth and me." He paused a moment and then added, "I was hoping once I got baptized, I might court you. I know I can't do that now. But if there was any girl I would want to marry, it would be you."

Surprised, she blinked. "You want to court me?"

"*Ja*, I'd ask you right now to marry me, if I could."

Gail covered his hand with hers, squeezing tight. "If I could say yes, I would," she whispered, careful that no other ears but his heard her words.

His gaze deepened. "Would you do something for me?"

She nodded.

"Kiss me, again. Please? Just one more time."

Throwing caution aside, Gail leaned forward. With no hesitation, Levi's warm mouth claimed hers. In that single precious moment, there was only the two of them as the rest of the world fell away.

Chapter Sixteen

After their kiss ended, Gail glanced around at the others in the cellar. No one had stirred. It would always be their secret.

They sat in companionable silence, each lost in their own thoughts. Regret hung between them. What would happen now? How could they ever be together? It was something Gail couldn't answer.

Breaking the stillness, Levi tipped his head. "Do you hear what I hear?"

Shaking off her thoughts, Gail tilted her head. The incessant howl outside had ceased, as had the attack of rain. "Nothing. I hear nothing," she murmured. "Is it over?"

"I think so."

Standing, Levi reached above his head, pressing the edge of the heavy metal. Rusty hinges protested with a screech. A thin sliver of light appeared between the door and the edge of the frame.

He peeked. "Sun's breaking the horizon. Storm's over."

Breathing in relief, Gail asked, "Can we go out?"

"I think so." He pushed the door open and looked around. She heard him catch his breath.

Gail stiffened. "What?"

"It's…" He hesitated, swallowing hard. "Bad."

Hurrying up the steps, Gail left the safety of the cellar and stepped back onto solid ground. The world she'd left behind and the one she returned to were two different things. The tornado had done its damage, tearing up the landscape. In the span of a night, her entire world had changed forever.

Gail's first thought was of the house. Running around to the front yard, she was relieved to see it remained standing. A few of the older trees around the perimeter had gone down, sending a spray of stray limbs through the front window.

She headed to the backyard and ran toward the barn and pens. Much to her relief, the animals appeared to have made it through all right. The rabbit hutches and chicken pens built against the far side of the barn still stood, as did the lean-to for the goats. Though muddy and wet, they had survived. Unfortunately, the barn itself had not fared so well. Part of the roof was entirely torn away, and the open side shed had crumbled.

Levi ran up beside her. "The horses!" he cried, hurrying to pull away the debris from the side door that would get them back inside.

Following close behind, Gail rushed to check the stalls. Pawing the ground and snorting, half a dozen skittish horses met her eyes. "They're on their feet."

"Good." Levi removed the plank holding the front double doors shut, pushing both open.

Together, they walked out. Across the barnyard, the

bunkhouse also appeared to have suffered minor damages. But that wasn't all. The tornado had turned over Levi's RV, completely totaling it.

As she trembled at the sight, a sob broke from Gail's throat. "Oh no!"

Levi's jaw hardened. If he had any thoughts about losing everything he and Seth owned, he kept them to himself.

"We need to check the cattle." Leaving his small trailer behind, he turned and disappeared back into the barn.

Gail hurried after him. Inside, she found him leading a horse out of its stall. Still a little skittish, the horse whinnied. "I'm going with you."

Saddling the horse with quiet efficiency, Levi brushed off her words. "No, you should stay here. The others will wake soon."

"I'm going, even if I have to saddle my own horse."

Brows knitting, Levi slipped a boot into the stirrup and heaved himself into the saddle. He held out a hand. "If you think you have to, then come on."

Accepting his help, Gail slipped a foot atop his, using the leverage he offered to take a seat behind him. Pulling herself close, she wrapped her arms around his waist. "Let's go."

Levi spurred the horse into action. "Giddyap!" Galloping through the barnyard, he pointed the horse in the pastureland's direction. The path of the tornado was clear, for it had torn through the fencing and created a gaping hole.

Gail held on tight as Levi urged the horse to run faster, taking them into the heart of the acreage where the cattle normally grazed. Near one of the watering tanks, the windmill had been mangled, reduced to broken planks and twisted metal. But that wasn't all. They saw cows scattered across the landscape, unmoving.

Levi reined the horse to a stop. He slid to the ground and handed Gail the reins as she slipped forward to take the saddle. He knelt near one of the cows. "They're gone."

Not trusting her eyes, Gail tapped the horse. The animal lifted its head and neighed in protest but kept going. Without really looking where she was going, she rode through the pasture. By her count, most of the cattle had perished.

Gaping in horror and disbelief, Gail squeezed her eyes shut. "Please, no."

The Longhorns, the pride of the Schroder ranch, were no more.

Tears stung her eyes, but she refused to let them fall. Senses reeling, she thought about the consequences of the damage. With no cattle to sell, there would be no money coming in. With no income, there was no way to make up the missed payments.

Soon, the bank could legally foreclose on the property and there would be nothing she could do to prevent it.

It is all gone, she silently lamented. *We are going to lose everything.*

Gail looked down at Levi. Dark circles from a sleepless night bruised his eyes. Grim-faced and pale, he looked up again at the sky. Now that the storm had blown out, it was as clear and blue as a crystal lake.

"What do we do now?"

He frowned. "We call a rendering plant and sell the

carcasses to them," he answered automatically. "You won't get a lot, but you will get something."

"How many do you think we lost?"

His brow furrowed. "Won't know for sure until we round up the stragglers. With the broken fences and acreage, might take a while to figure that out. Any loose cattle roaming have your brand, so we can reclaim them."

Hope flared. "Then there's a chance we can recover?"

"Depends on how hard you want to keep trying."

Gail dropped her gaze. "I—I'm not sure I can, Levi. *Daed*'s death, Mr. Slagel's theft, then this—"

She blinked, fighting back tears. So much had gone wrong this year. Everything was falling apart in front of her eyes.

Levi turned away to study the surrounding devastation. Then he said, "You should get back and let the others know what's happened."

"What about you?"

A shrug rolled off his shoulders. "I'll walk back. I need to check the fencing. No telling how much has been destroyed."

Reluctant to leave him, she nevertheless turned the horse around. "Go on," she urged, tapping her mount with a heel.

Spurred forward, the horse galloped across the plains.

Gail didn't glance back. She couldn't. All her hopes to save the ranch lay with the cattle, and now they were gone.

Along with the hope she'd nursed to carry on the Schroder legacy.

* * *

Hands on hips, Levi surveyed the remnants of his RV. Of all the items on the property, it was the worst hit. A total loss, there was no salvaging it. Everything he and Seth owned was inside. And now there was nothing. All they had was the clothes on their back and his truck. For the time being, he and Seth were homeless.

Holding Seth's hand, Gail stood nearby. "You and Seth can stay in your old room," she was saying. "We use it for storage, but Rebecca and Amity are cleaning it out. Mr. Weaver's also taken his pickup into town to pick up some new glass for the front window of the house. By this evening, things will be a little more normal."

Levi gave her half an ear. "Glad it's coming together."

Since the family had come out of the cellar and seen the devastation, everyone threw themselves into clearing away the debris. Shock passed quickly as the need to repair and restructure took over. Busy as an army of ants on the move, everyone had found something to do. There were still animals to care for, too.

As far as he could tell, instinct had moved the cattle to find shelter in the lower spots of the pasture, gathering in a tight bunch to shield the calves from the hail. The tornado had come straight through the herd, sending the animals into a panicked frenzy.

He shook his head. Once the radio station came back on air, the newsmen had reported the extent of the damage. The weather service confirmed the wind had reached over a hundred miles an hour, spawning a slew of tornadoes. Burr Oak and several surrounding towns had taken a lot of damage, not to mention the multiple farms throughout the region. Many people had lost homes and businesses. Thankfully, no one was killed, though livestock had not fared so well.

The Amish didn't believe in insurance. They relied on the collective community to lend a hand when times were hard. Given that the tornado had done a lot of damage to many families, resources would no doubt be stretched thin.

"Do you think that's okay?" Gail asked, trying to restart the conversation.

Levi transferred his gaze to her. "If you don't mind, Seth and I can stay in the bunkhouse until I can figure another RV. It has insurance, so I'll file a claim when there's time. It will be replaced. Might take a few weeks for them to settle. Meanwhile, it wouldn't be proper for us to move into the house with you and your sisters."

Gail acquiesced. "Of course, you are both welcome to stay there," she demurred.

Levi nodded. *"Gut."* It would be hard to keep his distance, but he resolved to do just that.

As soon as the insurance company sent a check, he'd be able to move on.

As for the ranch... Unless Gail could convince the bank to refinance the loan, Mr. Wilkins would most likely follow through with his threat to take the property. With the due date for payment rapidly approaching, there was no time to put the place up for sale and hope a buyer made an offer.

Seth broke away. "Daddy, can we find Mommy's book?"

Gail gave the boy a questioning look. "What is that? Perhaps it's something we can replace."

Though he didn't feel very encouraged, Levi offered his son a smile of reassurance. "I'm going to try to find it, bud," he said, eyeing the debris.

"Should you go inside?"

Levi considered the wreckage. "I should be able to at least reach Seth's bunk."

Passing through the remnants of the front door, Levi picked his way through the living room. The trailer was a jumbled mess. He navigated his way down the short hall and, entering their shared room, he kicked aside the rubble near the overturned bunks. It took him a minute to locate the white faux-leather photo album Seth wanted. Intertwined hearts and ribbons adorned the cover. Though dampened by the rain, it was still intact.

Levi's heart skipped a beat. It was his and Betheny's wedding album.

He didn't want to look, but couldn't help flipping open the cover. A myriad of images filled the pages. There were some of him from a few years ago. Others were of Betheny. There were some of Seth, too, after his birth. Pasted to the pages in vivid color were bits and pieces of his past.

A photo of him and Betheny on their wedding day gave rise to a lot of old feelings he'd believed were carefully packed away.

A closer look revealed something he'd never realized till today. Neither looked joyous. In fact, they both looked downright miserable.

I was never in love with Betheny, he thought.

Although his first impulse was to lie and tell Seth he couldn't find the photo album, Levi knew he couldn't do that to his young son. Even if his perceptions of his mother were hazy, Seth still loved his mother. Seth also believed Betheny had loved him. Whether he'd ever tell his son the truth remained to be seen. But for the time being he couldn't deny the child something he treasured.

Sighing, Levi closed the book. He looked around and saw a few of Seth's things that might be salvageable, including a few stuffed animals and some clothes. He picked through the items.

"Levi, are you all right?"

Hearing Gail's voice, he lifted his head. "Yes, I'm here."

"I'm coming in." Gail appeared shortly thereafter, tripping through the debris to join him. She offered a crooked smile. "I thought you could use some help."

"Where's Seth?"

"Florene took him to help with the goats."

"*Gut.* That'll take his mind off the RV and his stuff."

"Ezra just got back, too," she informed him. "He's brought word the church was damaged, too. The bishop's called a prayer session this evening, for those affected by the storm. Will you come?"

Levi bent, retrieving Seth's purple dinosaur. The thing was a soggy mess and would take days to dry. "No. If you don't mind, I think Seth and I will stay here. There's a lot of cleaning up to do."

She nodded. "We'll be leaving for town in about an hour, if you change your mind."

Even though the bishop had said he would give Levi's case due consideration, Levi didn't have much hope Bishop Harrison or his ministers would change their minds. In their eyes, he'd skipped out on his marriage vows. If he'd done that, they would probably be of the mind he wouldn't honor his vows to the church once he was baptized. The mistakes of his past had destroyed his future.

No one to blame but myself.

"Thank you, but I don't think I will. No reason for anyone to see my face around town right now."

Gail started to walk away and then stopped, visibly struggling with indecision. An awkward silence hung, widening the bridge between them.

"I know we will probably lose the property," she said quietly. "The cattle are gone, and we have no money. Taxes and other expenses have to be paid." Wrinkling her nose, she forced a laugh. "I hated taking care of cows anyway."

Shaking his head, Levi stepped forward. When Gail was working the cattle, he'd seen pride and determination on her face. True, the work was hard, but she'd carried it with grace, never complaining. Given a little more time, she'd have grown into a fine cattlewoman.

"Now you know in your heart that isn't true."

Momentarily going teary, Gail blinked hard. "You're right. Even though it was hard, I finally had the feeling I was getting ahead of the problems plaguing us." Stepping forward, she tilted back her head, gazing into his eyes. "I couldn't have done it without your help," she continued in a soft voice. "Since your arrival, you gave me so much hope and the courage to keep going."

Touched, Levi reached for her hand. "You gave me a lot, too. Without you, I wouldn't have found my faith. You and your sisters bought me back to *Gott*, and I am grateful. I know I can't go back to being Amish, but please know you will always hold a special place in my heart."

Lower lip trembling, Gail forced a smile. Sadness and longing lingered in the depths of her gaze. "I'll always love you, Levi Wyse," she murmured softly. "Always."

Chapter Seventeen

Levi spent a fitful night tossing and turning on the narrow bed in the bunkhouse. No matter how much he tried, sleep wouldn't come. After another hour of fighting to still his racing mind, he finally gave up. He swung his legs off the mattress and sat up.

The gentle glow of a digital clock lit the small room. The time read five fifty.

He glanced at the bed across from his own. Covered by a heavy quilt, Seth lay snuggled close to Sparky.

Moving with stealth so he wouldn't wake the boy, Levi rose. He pulled on his pants and shirt, picked up a small duffel bag he'd packed earlier and crept over the threshold, closing the door to the bedroom behind him. He didn't want Seth to wake up until after he left.

Entering the shared living room, he sat down to put on his socks and boots. For the last week, they had been living in the bunkhouse, occupying the space that would normally house the cowhands.

Levi walked to the stove. He turned on a burner, filled a kettle with water and set it to heat. He spooned instant coffee and sugar into a mug. When the water was boiling, he poured it over the mix and then added a dash of milk from the small fridge.

He sat down at the dining table and sipped his coffee. The kick of caffeine and sugar helped perk him up. He thought about eating breakfast, but the knots in his gut wouldn't allow it. He was too nervous. The coffee would have to keep him going awhile.

He glanced around the empty room. Housing intended for a bunch of rowdy cowboys wasn't the fanciest place he'd ever lived, but it wasn't uncomfortable. The bunkhouse had private bedrooms for sleeping. Two of the rooms were widened into a single larger living space for the Weavers. An open gathering room that included a kitchenette with propane appliances gave the hands a place to eat and relax.

Seth had taken the temporary move easily. The child liked living like a "real" cowboy.

Levi grimaced. Cowboying was the last thing he wanted Seth to pursue. He wanted Seth to go to school, learn a trade. Had his own father lived, Levi probably would have been a stonemason. It was a steady job, and a man could make a good enough living to support his family. That was what he wanted for Seth. Stability and a sense of belonging to the community. He might not be able to settle in Burr Oak, but there were plenty of other towns. Other places where no one knew him or anything about his past, Amish or otherwise.

Meanwhile, a man had to make a living, and he had a job to do. Once insurance took care of replacing the RV, he and Seth would leave town. The summer was young and there were many rodeos ahead.

But first, he intended to make things right with Gail and her family.

Finishing his coffee, Levi washed out the cup and set it in the rack to dry. He wanted to leave before Seth woke. If his son found out where he was going, he would want to go, too.

Duffel bag in hand, Levi slipped on his jacket and hat before stepping over the threshold, closing the door quietly so as to not disturb the rest of the sleeping household. The horizon was dark, the sun not quite ready yet to throw off its dark velvet cloak. The night sky above his head was crystal clear, spattered with stars that glowed like jewels. A light breeze caressed his stubbled face.

Tightening his grip on his bag, he passed the barnyard, heading toward the main house. His truck was parked outside, gassed up and ready to go. As he suspected, the kitchen windows were already lit with light. Since the storm, Gail had resumed breakfast duties, reclaiming her kitchen from Mrs. Weaver.

After the storm, the surviving cattle numbered about sixty, a number any good cowboy worth his salt could manage. The good news was three of the prime male sires and several young heifers had survived. It took nine months for cows to deliver, so new calves would not be born until next March or April. Given time, it would be possible to rebuild the herd.

Good news, but still a problem. With the barn severely damaged and no cull cattle to sell, the ranch still had a serious cash flow problem. And the threat of foreclosure was now too close for comfort.

Drawing a breath, Levi tapped on the screen door before opening it. "Hope I'm not bothering you."

Gail, busy at the counter, turned her head. "Of course not. Why would you?" Up to her elbows in flour, she threw him a smile. "I hope you're hungry. There's coffee on the stove and I'll be finished rolling out these biscuits in a minute."

Shaking his head, Levi removed his hat and sat down. Gail was her usual messy self, her plain gray dress and white apron all wrinkles and stains. A tear ran down one side of her apron. Flecks of flour dusted her chin and forehead. Defying the efforts of bobby pins, stray curls peeked out from under her *kapp*.

As he looked at her, Levi's breath caught in his throat. No matter what Gail might think about herself, she was beautiful in every way. She was kind, good-hearted and generous to a fault. She also treated his son as if he were her own.

I let this family down once, but I won't do that again. Time to step up and be a man.

"I had a cup of coffee at the bunkhouse," he said. "But if you don't mind, I'll fill a thermos to take with me on the drive to Fort Worth. Maybe you'd even consider making some sandwiches for me?"

Gail froze. "The competition. I'd forgotten."

Levi nodded. "You have a lot on your mind right now."

She shook her head. "The bank agent won't work with us to refinance the mortgage. They seem determined to take everything we have."

"That's not going to happen," Levi said. "I'll make sure of it."

Dusting off her hands, Gail placed them on her hips before shooting him a frown. "After seeing your friend seriously injured, I don't understand why you would even consider getting on one of those horses."

"I know the risks and I'm willing to take them." Determined to convince her it was the right thing to do, he continued, "If I get through the try-outs today, I get to compete for a share of that prize money I told you about. This rodeo will be the biggest event in the state for the Fourth of July, and I intend to be a part of it."

Clearly upset, Gail threw up her hands in frustration. "I saw a man thrown off a horse and almost lose his life right in front of my eyes." Her gaze traveled to his face. "That could be you some day."

Levi dug in his heels. He'd made up his mind and that was that.

"Unless I show up and win some money, you're going to lose your home. If I win enough, I can catch up the mortgage for you. It's the least I can do...before I leave."

Stepping forward, Gail pressed a warm palm against his scarred cheek. "Oh, you silly man," she said, blinking misted eyes. "I think it's admirable that you're willing to risk your life for this *familie*. But I can't expect you to do that, nor would I ask you to."

Savoring her touch, Levi covered her hand with his. "I have to do this. If not for you, then for Samuel. I owe him, and I intend to pay back my debt."

Letting her hand drop, Gail stepped back. "I guess I can't talk you out of the notion."

"I sound foolish, I know." He laughed. "At today's events, they whittle down the people who have been invited to enter. That's why the prize is so big. It's the best of the best. They will choose only ten competitors in each category. Three chances each, to make the best time."

"And if you don't qualify?"

"It's over. I'm out." Pausing, he hurried to add, "But I'm going to final, and then I'm going to win."

The fighting spirit left the depth of Gail's gaze. Her expression went blank. Mouth turned down, she returned to the cabinet, rummaging around for a thermos. "Let me get your food ready. Give me a few minutes. I have some cold ham that will make good sandwiches."

Unwilling to leave without having the final say, Levi grabbed Gail by the shoulders, turning her around to face him. Slipping his fingers beneath her chin, he angled back her head. "Don't give up, Gail. You're not going to lose the land your family has worked so hard to keep for generations. Not as long as I have breath in my body."

Trembling, Gail wrapped her arms around him. "Promise me you'll come back in one piece, Levi. Promise me."

"You have my word."

Hugging her tight, Levi pressed his lips to her forehead. How he wished he could hold her forever and never let her go.

Driven by nervous energy, Gail tried to get through the morning without breaking down in tears. Ever since Levi left for Fort Worth, driving through the front gate in his old pickup, she'd been unable to think straight. Her thoughts were jumbled, jumping from one idea to another. What if Levi got hurt? One wrong fall, one strike from an angry horse's hooves might injure him permanently. Worse, it could kill him.

Please, Gott, keep a hand of protection over him.

Keeping her thoughts to herself, she glanced at Seth. The boy sat at the kitchen table with sheets of art paper and Crayolas, blissfully unaware of the danger his father faced. It was not unusual for Levi to go to work before he woke. As far as Seth knew, his father was out on the range with the cattle.

Having finished breakfast and shooed her sisters out for the day, Gail tried to distract herself with cleaning. Whenever she had something on her mind, it was best to keep her hands busy. Otherwise, she'd sit and fret until she was a nervous wreck. Come noon, she'd entirely cleaned and rearranged the kitchen and living room until not a single speck of dust or lingering cobweb remained.

Exhausted, Gail treated herself to a cup of tea. She sat across from Seth and studied the child. As she watched him, so innocent and unaware, her heart squeezed a little. She still couldn't wrap her mind around the fact the child's mother hadn't wanted him. He was the sweetest little *boi*, generous and kind. Exactly like his father.

Finishing the page, Seth lifted his head. "See what I made for you," he said, turning the book to show her his work.

Gail glanced at the page. Like most children his age, Seth's style was still mostly abstract. Nevertheless, she could make out three figures and some animals under a bright rainbow.

"That's beautiful."

Seth pointed at one of the people with a hat. "That's *Datt*." His finger moved to a girlish figure in a dress. "That's you." He pointed to the tiny boy. "And that's me." He picked up a blue Crayola, marking across a fresh piece of paper. "I wish you could be my *mamm*," he blurted out.

Gail was caught by surprise. "You do?"

Face serious, Seth nodded. *"Ja."*

Not sure how to respond, she replied, "But you already have a mommy."

"Mommy is in heaven," Seth said, his face pinched with thought. "She can't take care of me and Daddy anymore like you do."

"I'm sure she would if she were here," Gail said, keeping her tone noncommittal.

Seth looked up at her through imploring eyes. "I want you to be my *mamm*," he said. "Forever and ever."

Gail's eyes misted, and her chin quivered. "I wish I could be your *mamm,* too. But since I can't, maybe I can be your Aunt Gail instead. Will that be okay?"

Seth slipped out of his chair and ran around the table. "Oh, yes!" Arms open, he threw himself at her, wrapping his small arms around her neck in a big hug. "And can Rebecca, Amity and Florene all be my aunts, too?"

"I am sure they would be happy to," she said, gathering the child up and pulling him into her lap. "We all love you and your *datt* very much."

"I wish we didn't have to go," Seth murmured, burying his head in the crook of her shoulder. "I want to stay."

Gail stroked the child's downy hair. "I wish you could stay, too," she murmured.

A knock at the front door interrupted.

Gail's brow furrowed. Who could that be? Levi was gone. As school was on summer hiatus, Rebecca was working part-time in her fiancé's butcher shop. Florene had thrown herself across her bed, glued to her smartphone. The Weavers had gone into town for the weekly supplies. She expected no guests.

Her heart seized. What if something had happened to Levi? The drive to Fort Worth was only two hours.

Texas highways sometime got crazy around the bigger cities. What if...?

Adrenaline flowing through her, Gail put Seth down. She rushed across the living room and pulled open the door. Her breath stalled.

A patrol car was parked in the drive, and Sheriff Miller stood at the door. "Good morning," he greeted. "I'm sorry to interrupt your day."

Butterflies taking flight inside her stomach, Gail stepped back. "Not at all, Evan. It's good to see you," she said. "Won't you please come in?"

"Actually, I haven't got time," he said. "I just wanted to stop by and let you know police in Oklahoma have picked up Walter Slagel. He's in jail now, awaiting transfer back to Texas."

Hardly daring to breathe, Gail forced herself to draw air into her lungs. "He's been caught?" she repeated, unable to believe her ears.

"Yes, he has. And there's more to tell," Sheriff Miller said. "Slagel had a duffel bag full of cash with him. It is not quite the amount he stole from you, but it's close. The legal process to return it takes time, but you will get your money back."

Gail's vision blurred as she took in the news. "Oh, thank *Gott*."

"You can thank the officer who recognized him from the BOLO we sent out," Sheriff Miller said.

"I certainly do." Still processing the good news, Gail smiled and offered her hand. Her prayers had been answered. "Thank you. Thank you so very much. This is the best news we could have gotten today."

Evan Miller tipped his hat. "My pleasure. I'll be in touch."

Turning on his heel, the sheriff strode to his patrol car and slid behind the wheel. He'd barely exited the drive before another car pulled in. The vehicle was unfamiliar, but the man who got out of the back seat was not. Because he was a busy man, Bishop Harrison preferred to hire a car and driver rather than try to make his calls around the community in a horse and buggy. As long as he didn't drive the vehicle, it was an accepted practice. Many Amish often hired drivers when traveling a long distance.

Wondering what would prompt the bishop's unexpected visit, Gail greeted him with a smile. "This is quite a surprise."

Bible in hand, Clark Harrison offered a brief smile. "*Guten nachmittag*, Gail," he greeted politely. "I hope I'm not disturbing anyone."

"Not at all," she said, and stepped back to allow him entry. "Please come in."

"I'm just visiting the families impacted by the tornado. I heard you also had damages."

"*Ja*, the house and the barn. Mostly the barn. The horses have no roof over their heads." Filling the teapot with fresh water, Gail set in on the stove. "May I offer you a cup of tea or coffee?"

"Tea would be lovely," he said, and took a seat near Seth. "How are you, young man?"

"*Ich bin* okay," Seth returned in perfect *Deitsch*.

Clark Harrison's brows rose. "*Wunderbar*," he said, ruffling the child's hair.

Gail poured a cup of fresh tea and set it in front of her visitor. She glanced toward Seth. Perhaps the boy should not listen to what adults might have to say.

"Seth, why don't you go upstairs and show Florene

your pretty drawings? I'm sure she would like to see them."

"Sure!" Bored with adult conversation, Seth grabbed a handful of pages and slipped out of his chair. His boots clattered on the wooden steps as he ascended the stairs.

"Your tea, sir."

Adding sugar, Bishop Harrison sipped his drink. "The reason I came is to assess the damages families suffered. The church has put together a coalition of volunteers who will help with homes and businesses that need rebuilding. I have also arranged deals with the suppliers of my hardware store to donate lumber and other necessary materials to complete the projects. We will do the work without cost to any family."

Freshening her own tea, Gail took a seat opposite him. "Oh, Bishop. That is wonderful. Such a blessing from *Gott*."

"I came to see if you and your sisters would be interested in donating a few dishes to feed the men as they move from job to job."

Gail dropped her gaze. "Of course. We will be happy to cook for them."

"Mmm, good." A pause. "Is Levi around? I'd like to speak to him if he has a moment."

"Levi is out." Unable to hold back her pent-up feelings, she blurted. "He told me he was turned away from rejoining the church."

"I see. Did he tell you why?"

Gail nodded. "*Ja*. He told me it was because he divorced his wife."

Setting his cup aside, Bishop Harrison cleared his throat. "Well, it behooves me to examine a person's past behaviors if they have left to live in the *Englisch* world awhile. Levi was away over a decade."

"Perfectly understandable. I don't disagree with your wisdom."

The Bishop gave his bearded chin a scratch. "True wisdom also means finding out all the facts before passing judgment."

"What do you mean?"

"I contacted a few people, to verify some details about Levi's past. It might be true he divorced his wife, but two facts stand out very starkly," Clark Harrison explained. "The first is that his wife was a danger to those around her, especially their young son. It is a parent's duty to protect the innocent, and Levi was doing all the law allowed in order to accomplish that."

"I see. And what is the second?"

"As he didn't marry in a church and his *Englisch* wife is deceased, my ministers and I agree there is no reason he can't rejoin the church. I believe he is sincere in his repenting and wants to make a better life for himself and his son."

Hope sprang up, circling Gail's heart. "Are you saying Levi can be baptized?" she said in a trembling voice, close to tears all over again.

Bishop Harrison nodded. "*Ja*. Of course, he will still have to take the baptismal classes, as everyone does before making such a life-altering decision, but I see no issues preventing him from rejoining our community."

Joy lifted her spirit. "Levi didn't think he'd be forgiven for what he did."

Clark Harrison took a sip of his tea. "Well, the Lord happens to be in the business of forgiving people. Once he rejoins the church, Levi's past is just that. In the past."

Inside, her soul soared. The dream she'd watched turn to ashes came sparking back to life, rising like a phoenix from the flames. All she ever wanted—to marry Levi Wyse and have his *kinder*—loomed as an actual possibility.

"Where is Levi? I would like to tell him the good news."

Her joy quickly drizzled away. "Oh, Bishop, Levi's gone to Fort Worth to compete in a rodeo there."

Clark Harrison's brows rose. "I see."

"It's not what you think," Gail said, and hurried to explain. "A few months ago, our manager stole money from the ranch account. He took every cent we had and disappeared."

The bishop nodded. "Is that why Sheriff Miller was here?"

"The sheriff came to tell us that Walter Slagel has been caught—and they've retrieved the stolen money."

"I had no idea you faced such troubles, my child. If you had only come to me with your issues, perhaps I could have helped."

Gail dropped her gaze. "I was so ashamed I let that man steal from us, Bishop. I didn't know what to do. Levi, bless his soul, was a saving grace. Everything was going so well. And then the storm happened, killing the cattle we planned to sell to keep the bank from taking our home." Pausing she took a breath. "Levi's trying to win the money he thinks we need."

"I admire his fortitude," Bishop Harrison said.

"I didn't want him to go. Not after seeing his friend injured at the rodeo last week."

"I heard about that tragic accident."

Gail pressed a hand to her stomach. "What if it hurts or kills him? Where would that leave his *sohn*?" She tried to find more words, but fear stalled her tongue.

"I understand your concerns." The bishop took one of her hands in his. "If you like, we will pray for Levi's safety."

Gail shook her head. "Bishop, may I beg of you to do something for me?"

The kindly older man gave her a nod. "Of course."

"Please, take me to Fort Worth. We need to find Levi and stop him before he gets on one of those broncs."

Chapter Eighteen

Riding in the back of the car with the bishop, Gail tried not to focus on the traffic around Fort Worth. Though it would be hard for people to believe it, she rarely traveled far from Burr Oak. The city, with its massive buildings and soaring off-ramps, was mind-boggling, filled with so many people all determined to go somewhere.

Securely fastened with a safety belt, Gail didn't feel one bit better. Cars and trucks might be more convenient for long-distance travel, but she believed she'd always love the slow and steady pace of a horse and buggy. As for Burr Oak, the tiny Texas town suited her fine, having enough services and necessities to keep it from being labeled the boonies.

"You all right?" Bishop Harrison asked.

Gail offered a weak nod. She wouldn't say it out loud, but the automobile made her dizzy. "I'm fine," she said, forcing herself to keep her breaths steady. It didn't help that her nerves were all sharp edges.

What if we get there and Levi's already hurt?

Gail quickly banished the notion.

"Thank you for giving up your day to bring us," she said. "I'm so very grateful."

Bishop Harrison waved a hand. "Been a long time since I've gotten out of town. I rather enjoy a long ride. And I haven't been to a rodeo in ages." He chuckled. "I used to go with my own father when I was a boy. It will be nice to revisit some old memories."

Settled between the adults in his car seat, Seth looked up. "My *datt* rides broncs. The horses, they buck really hard."

"*Ja*, Seth, I know," Gail said, squeezing his little hand. Her own were cold as the arctic chill invading her heart and lungs. Anxiety beat double time through her veins. Images of the man injured in the Eastland rodeo kept replaying in her mind's eye.

As if reading her mind, Seth looked grim. A dark shadow touched the boy's face, erasing pride. "I hope the horse don't hurt him like it hurt Mister Shane."

Gail shivered. Seth, too, had been in the audience that night. He'd seen the accident and it had clearly affected him.

"That's why we're going to tell him to stop."

Seth bobbed his head agreeably. "I think *Datt* should come home. The cows miss him."

"Where exactly are we going?" the bishop's *Englisch* driver asked, navigating the van through traffic. "I need a destination."

Mind freezing, Gail blanked.

"I—I don't know," she stammered, anxiety scattering her wits. "All I know is it's in Fort Worth." She'd been so upset with Levi's plan that she hadn't gotten a single detail.

"No problem, I'll find out." Reaching in a pocket, Bishop Harrison pulled out a smartphone.

Gail gaped. She had no inkling the bishop himself would use one.

He noticed her stare. "This is definitely an emergency." He launched a verbal search app. Within seconds, he had an address. "Take us to the Sports and Livestock Arena," he told the driver, giving him the address.

The driver punched it into the GPS on his dash. "Got it. On our way." A few minutes later, he turned on to an exit.

Soon the entertainment center came into view. After paying the parking fee, the driver found a spot. A multitude of monster diesel trucks and horse trailers filled the parking lot of a massive, fenced corral overhung by a rectangular domed roof designed to protect it from the rain during the outdoor events.

The driver pulled into a parking space lined along the iron security fencing. "Here you go, Bishop. I'll wait here."

"Hopefully, we won't be long," Bishop Harrison said, opening the car door.

Gail unlatched her seat belt and then unbuckled Seth. Accompanied by the bishop, they hurried toward the entry gate. A uniformed security agent stopped their progress.

"Is this the tryouts for the rodeo next weekend?" Gail asked, not sure exactly what to ask.

The tall man nodded. "Yes, but it's not open to the public."

Gail's heart dropped to her feet. "Then we can't go in?"

"Not unless you're with one of the competitors," he stated, shaking his head.

Thinking fast, Gail tightened her grip on Seth's hand. "Levi Wyse is competing today. This is his son, Seth. I am bringing him to his father. I'm his sitter," she added for good measure. "And this is Bishop Harrison. He has some news that Levi needs to hear."

Seth seconded her words. "My *datt* is a cowboy," he proudly informed the man.

Mistaking the bishop's clothes for funeral attire, the man said, "I hope there's not an emergency."

The bishop chuckled. "Only if you consider salvation and the saving of a soul an emergency."

The security agent checked his clipboard. "That guy is here," he said, and made a quick decision. "Go ahead." He opened the gate. "Just don't say it was me who let you inside if there's any trouble."

Relieved they had made it past security, Gail tugged Seth toward the massive arena. Competitors waiting for their event milled around, preparing their animals for the events to come. Surrounded by iron fencing, a series of gates kept the horses and bulls penned in place until it was time for release.

Locating a man with a tablet and a badge that read "Judge," Gail tugged his arm. "Excuse me, sir. I'm looking for Levi Wyse. He is competing today."

Consulting his tablet, the man nodded. "Levi's up for his third run in just a few minutes." He pointed. "Just over there."

"Danke." Searching through the cowboys milling around, she spotted Levi talking to another man. The bishop hung back, letting her go ahead.

Spotting his father, Seth broke away from her grip. *"Datt!"* Limbs in motion, he rushed to his father and wrapped his arms around Levi's waist. "I'm so happy to see you."

Shocked by the appearance of his child, Levi knelt and gripped Seth's shoulders. "How did you get here?"

Before the boy could speak, Gail hurried up. "Levi, praise *Gott* we found you."

Levi stood. "I'll be right back," he said to the man. Pulling her and Seth aside so they could talk in private, he gave her a strange look. "What are you all doing here?"

"I want you to stop this nonsense and come home," Gail blurted, taking in his battered appearance. When he'd left that morning, Levi was spick-and-span from head to toe. Now his clothes were badly wrinkled and caked with dirt. He looked like he'd hit the ground hard several times. He was dressed in well-used chaps and with spurs on his boots, and a single, fingerless glove covered his right hand.

Levi glanced over his shoulder. "I'm almost up for my third run," he said. "This is the one. If I make the numbers, I'm in."

"Putting your life in danger for money isn't worth the risk."

Tipping back his hat, Levi rubbed his temple. "I need to do this, Gail. No matter the consequences."

"Levi, I have something to tell you."

He hushed her. "I know what you're going to say. But the Bible also says you can do all things through *Him* who strengthens you. I have given this to the Lord, and I am putting it in *His* hands. Whatever the outcome, it's *His* will."

Seeing the set of his jaw and the glint of determination in his eyes, Gail raised her gaze to his. "If that's what you feel you have to do, then I won't try to stop you."

"Wyse, you're up," a man barked, interrupting.

Levi waved a hand to acknowledge the call. "Coming," he answered back. "One minute."

"Go." No matter the outcome, she had to support his decision. "May the Lord ride with you."

A slow grin turned up one corner of his mouth. "Do I get a hug?"

Gail crossed her arms over her chest. Not because she didn't want to throw herself in his arms and squeeze him tight, but because the extensive number of men surrounding them embarrassed her. It wouldn't be proper to express affection in front of all these prying eyes.

"I expect you to come back in one piece," she said. "And then you'll get your hug."

Seth had no such reservations. "I know you can beat that bronc," he enthused, jumping up and down.

"You can bet I will do my best, son." Levi caught his boy in a bear hug, lifting him off his feet. "And for you," he said to Gail.

"Wyse," a voice called again. "Now or never."

Lowering Seth, Levi gave a final, crooked smile. "Take good care of him." Turning, he hurried away.

Gail stood rooted in her place.

A tap on her shoulder caught her attention. "I believe we can watch over there." The bishop pointed to a seating area. Having stayed at a discreet distance, he'd observed all that happened.

Legs trembling, Gail nodded. "Thank you."

Leading her to a seat, Bishop Harrison sat beside her. "I know you are worried. But there's something that pushes men into doing difficult or dangerous things, even when there's a risk of injury or death."

Smoothing her skirt across her lap, Gail shook her head. "I guess I will never understand."

Bishop Harrison patted her arm. "We men want to know we're strong and can take care of our women and children. This is Levi's way of saying he will take care of you and Seth, even if it kills him. Your job is to support his decision."

There was no more time for conversation.

Searching with an anxious gaze, Gail spotted Levi. He climbed over the fence and entered the small area keeping the horse pinned into place. A few men kept the massive beast settled as he climbed on to the wild animal's back.

An announcement came over the loudspeaker. "Next up is Levi Wyse." The male voice went on, giving out a few facts and statistics about Levi's career.

Hearing his father's name, Seth cheered loudly. "That's my *datt*!" He called to anyone who cared to listen. Face beaming, he stood up in his chair so he could better see the event about to take place. "He's a rodeo king!"

A few spectators sitting nearby chuckled over his enthusiasm.

"You tell your daddy to bring it on home!" one man called out, clapping.

Egged on, Seth clenched his fists above his head. "You can beat that old bronc!"

Gail glanced up at the boy. Having watched his father compete before, Seth didn't seem a bit concerned. All he focused on was the excitement brewing.

All she focused on was the outcome. Blinking back tears, she watched anxiously as Levi raised his left hand and nodded.

* * *

Sitting astride the bronc, Levi took a breath to calm his racing pulse. This was it. The moment he'd been waiting for. Make the magic number in the scores, and he'd be in next week's rodeo. Fail, and he'd be walking out a loser.

And the Schroder sisters would lose their home.

Not going to happen.

"So help me *Gott*," he murmured.

With only seconds to spare, Levi gazed toward the audience. He didn't see Gail, but he knew she'd be watching every second of his ride.

Tightening his grip and setting his knees against the sides of the horse, he clenched his jaw and gritted his teeth. His heart jumped to his throat, and his pulse beat at his temples. Anxiety shot into the red zone.

"Let's do this."

A bell rang out, clear and loud. Two waiting cowboys pulled the gate open.

Set free, the wild horse bolted, leaping straight into the air, a tangle of sinew and sheer muscle in motion. Levi held on for dear life, mentally counting the seconds he needed. After the third or fourth buck, he was not sure he could last much longer. Every bone in his body rattled. Heart pumping a mile a minute, he felt the blood rush through his veins.

Giving a final, manic leap, the horse sent Levi flying straight into the air. Losing his grip, he slammed into the nearby fence. He lost his ability to breathe before crumbling to the hard ground.

Levi landed on his side and lay there, unable to move. The onlookers gasped, even as two men on horses galloped in to control the roiling bronc. With the help of the rodeo clowns, they were able to distract the horse and lead it away.

Refusing to panic, Levi forced himself to breathe, taking in much-needed oxygen to clear his rattled brain. He wiggled his fingers and then his toes. As far as he could tell, he was in one piece and nothing was broken.

Reaching up, he grabbed onto the fence and pulled himself to his feet. The ride had lasted only seconds, but it felt like an eternity. Feeling his left ankle give out, he limped into the arena. Aside from a sprain, he'd survived the challenge intact.

The onlookers roared, cheering furiously.

Reclaiming his smashed hat, Levi signaled he was all right. A couple of competitors came in to lead him out of the arena to safety. As he walked, a voice came over the loudspeaker, "Levi Wyse, ladies and gentlemen. Judges will announce the score soon."

Just like that, it was over. Win or lose, he'd done what he came to do.

Caught between excitement and the anxiety that he'd upset Gail, he looked around outside the gate. Both Gail and his son waited nearby.

Seth burrowed in, grasping his legs. "You beat that bronc, Daddy!"

Ruffling Seth's hair, he gave Gail a crooked grin. "So how about that hug now?"

A reluctant smile turned up Gail's fine lips. "All right. But just this once." Leaning in, she circled his neck with her arms, squeezing tight. "You scared me so much," she whispered in his ear.

Levi nodded. "I know, and I'm sorry. I didn't mean to frighten you."

She let him go and stepped back. "I'm never going through that again," she said in a calm voice.

Before he could reply, a hearty hand clapped him on the shoulder. "Congratulations, my boy. You did well."

Recognizing the voice, Levi turned. "Bishop Harrison, what are you doing here?"

"I came to see you this morning, but you weren't home," the bishop replied jovially. "When Gail told me where you were, I offered her a ride to Fort Worth."

"Thank you for bringing her and Seth, Bishop. I appreciate it."

"I don't mean to impede on your celebration," he continued. "But I would like to speak with you when things have calmed down a bit."

Mouth going bone-dry, Levi felt his insides tighten with painful anxiety. Well, that didn't sound promising. He swallowed down the lump in his throat. "Whatever you've got to say, you might as well spit it out."

"Well, you can stop looking like I've just kicked your favorite dog and burned your crops," Clark Harrison said, adjusting the black frames of his thick glasses. "What I want to tell you is that I'm still planning to put the Amish back in you—that is, if you'll start coming to church again."

Levi struggled to find his tongue. "You—you mean I can be baptized?"

"*Ja*. My ministers and I have revisited your case and after going over the matter, we have ruled that you were acting in the best interests of your *familie*." Bishop Harrison glanced from Levi to Seth. "I know your heart is good and that you care for your son very much. I am honored you would want to raise Seth in the church, and hope that he, too, will one day want to join the community."

Emotion squeezed Levi's throat. "Thank you, Bishop," he said, reaching out to shake Clark Harrison's hand with grateful enthusiasm. "I intend to raise him to lead a good Christian life."

"*Gut*. Then I expect to see you both in church this Sunday." Clark Harrison fished out a pocket watch. "Well, as much as I have enjoyed my time in Fort Worth, the day is getting away." He looked to Gail. "I trust you will ride home with Levi?"

She smiled. "Yes. Thank you for bringing us."

"My pleasure." Bishop Harrison tipped his hat and bade them all goodbye. Weaving his way through the crowd, he disappeared.

The bishop had no more than disappeared from sight when another man holding a clipboard jogged up.

"Your numbers, Levi," he said, handing over a sheet of paper. "The judges gave you a score of ninety-five. You've set a new record. Congratulations. You've also qualified for next week's rodeo. You've hit the big time." He walked away, leaving everyone dumbstruck.

Levi looked at Gail and then back to the paper in his hand. He was speechless. The numbers on the page listed him as a finalist. He blinked several times to make sure he'd read it right.

Heartbreak in her gaze, Gail stared at him. "I'm so happy for you, Levi," she said, giving his arm a squeeze. "I guess you're going to want to compete next week-end."

Levi searched her face. "Why wouldn't I? This is my chance to get the money you need."

"You don't have to," Gail said, adding a wide smile.

"Sheriff Miller came by the house earlier. The police caught Mr. Slagel. He had the money with him."

Disbelief widened his eyes. "You're kidding? That's wonderful."

"He said we will get back most of what was stolen." She reached for his hand and clasped it in hers. "I want you to come home and help me rebuild the herd. I can't do it without you."

A grin split his face. "Are you trying to hire me?"

Frustrated, Gail blurted out, "*Nein*. I'm asking you to marry me, Levi Wyse." The words pushed past her lips before she could stop them.

He gave her a cockeyed look. "Did you just propose?"

A rush of heat flooded her cheeks. She couldn't believe what she'd just said. "I—I—" she stammered helplessly.

Laughing, Levi made a sudden decision. He tossed the paper away.

Gail's eyes widened. "What are you doing?"

"I'm saying yes. But we have to do this the right way. I'm the one who is supposed to do the asking." Then, untangling himself from Seth's hold, he placed his hands on her shoulders. "Gail Schroder, will *you* marry *me*?"

Gail burst into tears. "Oh, Levi. I thought I would never hear you say those words." She wiped at her eyes.

He pulled her closer. Placing a gentle kiss on her forehead, he looked down into her eyes. "I hope that means you are saying yes."

Gail cried harder. "*Ja*," she said, and laughed through her tears. "*Tausendmal, ja.*" A thousand times yes.

Epilogue

Two weeks later

Busy working at the kitchen counter, Gail wiped the back of her hand across her perspiring brow. She'd spent the entire morning baking fresh bread, then cutting up thick slabs of ham for the sandwiches she made. She needed at least two dozen, maybe more.

She glanced up to check the time. The clock read ten minutes to twelve, and a lot of hungry men would expect lunch soon.

"Is the lemonade ready?"

Spatula in hand, Rebecca scooped freshly baked cookies onto a waiting plate. "It's chilling in the fridge now, with plenty of ice."

Gail nodded her approval. "The men have been working on the barn since sunrise. They're going to be famished."

"I still can't believe Levi won so much money," Florene said, adding mustard and mayonnaise to the bread Gail had laid out before adding the ham. She stacked the sandwiches neatly on a waiting tray.

"Hard to believe, but it's true," Gail said. The surprise still had her reeling.

Even though Levi didn't compete in The Big Texan, he'd received a letter in the mail, recognizing his record-breaking ride at the finals. A check for fifty thousand dollars was included, part of the bonus prize all finalists shared. There was enough money to catch up on the mortgage payments and repair the barn. It would also tide them over until the court ordered the return of the money Walter Slagel had stolen. The criminal proceedings still lay ahead, and Gail was ready to testify against the man who had come close to costing her family everything they owned.

For now, the focus was on rebuilding the herd. To celebrate the joining of their families, she and Levi had created a new brand, incorporating the *S* and the *W* of their names. The Schroder-Wyse Ranch would go on.

Thinking of all that had happened, Gail smiled to herself. Once she and Levi had officially tied the knot, they would become a proper family. Faith and the power of love had brought them together. Their path had been a rocky one, fraught with tragedy and trying times. But hard work and plenty of prayer had delivered many blessings. Hopefully, the Lord would also bless her and Levi with many *kinder* of their own.

"We'd better get this food out there," Rebecca said, heading for the back door with a tray of her famous oatmeal raisin cookies.

"I know the men must be hungry," Gail said, picking up the tray of sandwiches while Florene grabbed the lemonade from the fridge.

The three of them walked outside.

Amity was directing a couple of *youngies* to set the picnic tables and benches under the shadiest trees.

"Now set them just there," she ordered briskly, before covering them with a pretty tablecloth and putting out a stack of paper plates and cups. Plastic coolers sat nearby, full to the brim with bottled water on ice.

The wives of the workers arrived in their buggies. Delighted with the arrival of his friends, Seth ran to play with the other children. The sound of laughing children and chattering voices filled the air.

Putting down her tray, Gail glanced up at the sky. The July day was warm, but not blistering. The breeze kicked up a skittering of clouds, scenting the air with the promise of rain.

"Through rain or shine, *Gott* will keep us safe," she murmured, sending up a silent prayer of thanks.

Standing close by, Rebecca smiled. "Amen."

At the strike of noon, the men laid aside their tools and headed into the backyard for their meal. Though it might seem an incredible feat, a crew of men could raise a new barn within ten hours. Every man there had volunteered his time as an early wedding gift.

Levi walked among the group. No longer clad in Western-style clothes, he dressed in the same dark trousers, boots and white shirt that the other men wore. As soon as he completed his studies, Bishop Harrison would perform his baptism, bringing Levi back into the fold of the Amish community. Not long afterward, he and Gail would stand before the entire congregation and share their vows.

Gail's heart swelled with pride as he closed the distance between them. She'd never been happier or felt more at peace. Levi was hers and nothing would ever part them.

"And there's the prettiest girl I know," he said as a greeting.

Flushing, Gail shook her head. "And the happiest." She'd smiled every minute since he'd proposed. And once the bishop pronounced them to be man and wife, she didn't ever intend to stop.

Reaching out, Levi caught her hands in his and leaned forward. "I'd love to steal a kiss, but there's too many people around," he whispered so only she could hear.

Gail felt her cheeks heat with a blush. "There will be time for kisses after we are wed."

Stepping back, his smile widened. "I hope you got what you wanted."

"Of course, I did," she said, and tossed him a saucy wink. "You forget, I'm not only Amish, but I'm also a Texan. And Texas women always get their man."

* * * * *

Dear Reader,

Thank you all for visiting Burr Oak, Texas. I know many people wouldn't connect the Amish and Texas, but it is true that the Lone Star state has a few small Amish settlements. Although Burr Oak is a fictional version of an Amish town, I have done my best to adhere to the traditions of the Plain folks in a respectful and realistic manner.

I hope you all enjoyed Levi and Gail's story. Although Levi has big dreams for himself in the rodeo, eventually his heart turns toward his Amish heritage and the girl he left behind. Having strayed, he rediscovers his lost faith and how God can show a man his true path, especially after the ways of the world have lead him astray. Gail, too, learns a lesson. Though she is strong in her faith, she wavers when faced with challenges in her life. Together, they both learn to put their trust in God and are rewarded with many blessings.

I hope you will all want to visit Burr Oak again soon.

Sending love and light,
Pamela Desmond Wright

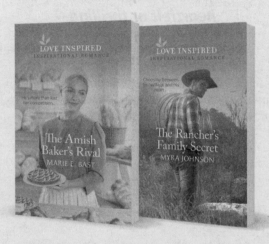

Get 4 FREE REWARDS!

We'll send you 2 FREE Books plus 2 FREE Mystery Gifts.

Love Inspired books feature uplifting stories where faith helps guide you through life's challenges and discover the promise of a new beginning.

FREE
Value Over
$20

YES! Please send me 2 FREE Love Inspired Romance novels and my 2 FREE mystery gifts (gifts are worth about $10 retail). After receiving them, if I don't wish to receive any more books, I can return the shipping statement marked "cancel." If I don't cancel, I will receive 6 brand-new novels every month and be billed just $5.24 each for the regular-print edition or $5.99 each for the larger-print edition in the U.S., or $5.74 each for the regular-print edition or $6.24 each for the larger-print edition in Canada. That's a savings of at least 13% off the cover price. It's quite a bargain! Shipping and handling is just 50¢ per book in the U.S. and $1.25 per book in Canada.* I understand that accepting the 2 free books and gifts places me under no obligation to buy anything. I can always return a shipment and cancel at any time. The free books and gifts are mine to keep no matter what I decide.

Choose one: ☐ **Love Inspired Romance Regular-Print**
(105/305 IDN GNWC)

☐ **Love Inspired Romance Larger-Print**
(122/322 IDN GNWC)

Name (please print)

Address _____ Apt. #

City _____ State/Province _____ Zip/Postal Code

Email: Please check this box ☐ if you would like to receive newsletters and promotional emails from Harlequin Enterprises ULC and its affiliates. You can unsubscribe anytime.

Mail to the **Harlequin Reader Service:**
IN U.S.A.: P.O. Box 1341, Buffalo, NY 14240-8531
IN CANADA: P.O. Box 603, Fort Erie, Ontario L2A 5X3

Want to try 2 free books from another series? Call 1-800-873-8635 or visit www.ReaderService.com.

LIR21R2

*Newly guardian to her twin nieces, Hannah Antonicelli
is determined to keep her last promise to her late
sister—that she'll never reveal the identity of their
father. But when Luke Hutchenson is hired as a
handyman at her work and begins to bond with the little
girls, hiding that he's their uncle isn't easy...*

Read on for a sneak peek at
Finding a Christmas Home *by Lee Tobin McClain!*

On Wednesday after work, Hannah drove toward home, the
twins in the back seat, and tried not to be nervous that Luke
was in the front seat beside her.

"I really appreciate this," he said. His car hadn't started this
morning, and he'd walked the three miles to Rescue Haven.

Of course, Hannah had insisted on driving him home. What
else could she do? It was cold outside, spitting snow, and he
was her next-door neighbor.

"I hate to ask another favor," he said, "but could you stop by
Pasquale's Pizza on the way?"

"No problem." She took a left and drove the two blocks to
the only nonchain pizza place in Bethlehem Springs.

He jumped out, and she turned back to check on the twins,
trying not to watch Luke as he headed into the shop. He was
good-looking, of course. Kind, appreciative and strong. And he
had the slightest swagger in his walk that was masculine and
appealing.

But he was also about to go visit his brother, Bobby, if he kept his promise to his ailing father. And when she'd heard about that visit, it had been a wake-up call: she shouldn't get too close with him. The fewer chances she had to spill the beans about Bobby being the twins' father, the better.

He came out of the pizza shop quickly—he must have called ahead—carrying a big flat box and a white bag. What would it be like if this was a family scenario, if they were Mom and Dad and kids, stopping for takeout on the way home from work?

She couldn't help it. Her chest filled with longing.

He climbed into her small car, juggling the large flat box to make it fit without encroaching on the gearshift.

She had to laugh at the size of his meal. "Hungry?"

"Are you?" He opened the box a little, and the rich, garlicky fragrance of Pasquale's special sauce filled the car.

Her stomach growled, loudly.

"Pee-zah!" Addie shouted from the back seat.

"Peez!" Emmy added, almost as loud.

"That's just cruel," she said as she pulled the car back onto the road and steered toward Luke's place. "You're tempting us. I may have to order some when I get these girls home."

"No, you won't," he said. "This is for all of us. The least I can do is feed you, after you drove me around."

Her stomach gave a little leap, and not just about the prospect of pizza. Why was he inviting her to have dinner with him? Was there an ulterior motive? And if there was, would she mind?

Don't miss
Finding a Christmas Home *by Lee Tobin McClain,*
available October 2021 wherever
Love Inspired books and ebooks are sold.

LoveInspired.com

IF YOU ENJOYED THIS BOOK, DON'T MISS NEW EXTENDED-LENGTH NOVELS FROM LOVE INSPIRED!

In addition to the Love Inspired books you know and love, we're excited to introduce even more uplifting stories in a longer format, with more inspiring fresh starts and page-turning thrills!

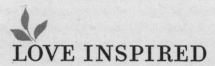

LOVE INSPIRED

Stories to uplift and inspire.

Fall in love with Love Inspired—inspirational and uplifting stories of faith and hope. Find strength and comfort in the bonds of friendship and community. Revel in the warmth of possibility, and the promise of new beginnings.

LOOK FOR THESE LOVE INSPIRED TITLES ONLINE AND IN THE BOOK DEPARTMENT OF YOUR FAVORITE RETAILER!